My Sugar in Sugar Land

DEE OSAH

MY SUGAR IN SUGAR LAND

For information, visit:
Dee Osah (www.deeosah.com)

Edited by Ineye Komo
Book Cover design by Austin M. Pennington (Redbridge Graphics)
Book Formatting by Derek Murphy @Creativindie
ISBN: 978-1-962485-01-2

First Edition: July 2024

10 9 8 7 6 5 4 3 2 1

ACKNOWLEDGEMENTS

Most of all, we would like to express our gratitude to our lovely daughters, J&J, for their inspiration, hugs, and kisses throughout the journey of writing this book. We love you tremendously and hope one day you'll come to love this book as much as we loved writing it.

A special thanks to our editor, Ineye Komo, for believing in our story and providing constructive criticism that strengthened the narrative. Your dedication to shaping this manuscript is much appreciated.

This book would not be the same without the exceptional cover design by Austin Pennington. You're the real MVP for providing such captivating illustrations and bearing with all our revisions.

Finally, to our dear readers, we are honored and grateful for all the time you spent with us. Thank you for giving our characters a home in your imagination.

1

After the scandal blew his career to pieces, Silas Harry left Nigeria to escape the bad press. His new movie Red Avenue had tanked days before he knocked out the wannabe gangster he'd caught breaking into his house. He landed in Houston on a Friday afternoon and scanned the long line of cars waiting outside the airport. His best friend Kay pulled up to the curb in a silver Benz SUV.

Silas didn't hurry to get into the car. Since arriving at the airport, he noticed a man with big shades, a black baseball hat, and a small scar–tribal mark on his right cheek. Every time he'd tried to get a good look at the stranger, the man had covered his face with his phone like a tourist taking pictures or looking for directions.

Kay stepped out of the Benz to help Silas with his bag. "Great disguise," Kay said, looking like he might laugh. "Haven't seen you with glasses since law school."

"You're late," Silas said. "What if someone saw me?" He slipped into the car and looked past Kay through the driver's window to the pickup area. The strange man was gone. Silas shook his head. Maybe he was being paranoid, and the man wasn't following him after all.

"Aren't you thinking you're more famous than you really are?" Kay asked, watching his window as if wondering what Silas was looking at. "Oh wait, you did just beat up a reporter, so you might be going viral here too."

"He was a thug," Silas corrected, edge creeping into his voice. Social media had spun the story to make the guy appear like an innocent reporter looking for a scoop.

It took Kay a while to wade through airport traffic and get on the freeway. Silas finally relaxed against the headrest. Even with Maxwell Johnson's wide connections, it would take some time before the goons found him in Houston. The stranger at the airport was probably a coincidence.

"Thanks for looking out," Silas said. He'd last seen Kay at the Olympics six years ago, where they had met up in Beijing to watch the Super Eagles lose in the football final. When Kay had called to ask if Silas would be his firstborn child's godfather, Silas told him he didn't deserve the honor, but Kay's wife insisted it couldn't be anyone else.

"I saw your...last week." Kay looked like he hated what he wanted to say. "She asked about you and I told her you were fine."

"She's not why I came here," Silas said. No matter how many times he told Kay not to talk about her, Kay always brought her up, never quite understanding why Silas couldn't let go of the past.

Silas looked outside the window as the SUV zipped past other cars on the highway, skyscrapers and giant billboards. Just like they said, everything was bigger in Texas. The wide road lanes were smooth. He would love driving here. He could take a road trip to Dallas for a Cowboys game. No, wrong time of the year. Besides, laying low meant avoiding any place where thousands of people gathered.

"We're here," Kay said.

Silas rubbed his eyes. He had fallen asleep. He was sleeping more these days, but for the past week, he would close his eyes and when he opened them again, it was as if he hadn't slept at all.

In no time, Silas pulled out of the car rental lot with a Kia SUV, a far cry from the glitzy rides he owned back home. With a promise to call Kay in the morning, Silas waved goodbye and set his GPS for the hotel he'd hurriedly booked a few days ago. He needed a shower, some sleep, and lots of liquor. Then he could get to work unraveling the mess he had made of his life. After finally getting the lead role in a big movie, he was so caught up in the sky that he forgot to watch out for the landmines on the ground.

The Marriott was near the highway, and before long, Silas checked into his room and crashed on the bed to take a short nap. He was so tired that he slept right through dinner and woke up around two in the morning.

Settling down on the pullout couch, he watched a movie, the events of the past month still flashing through his mind. By the time the movie ended, his stomach was growling. The past days had been so draining that he hadn't eaten much. He changed into fresh clothes and left his room. As he neared the front desk in the lobby, he saw the man and ducked into the adjoining hallway. The same man from the airport, with the tribal scar on his right cheek, was talking to the woman at the counter.

"Have you seen him?" the stranger asked in a thick Nigerian accent, holding up his phone to the woman. "We're supposed to meet here. I forgot his room number and haven't been able to reach him on his phone."

Silas rushed back to his room. 'Disgraced Silas Harry found in Houston,' the headline would read. But that man didn't look like a reporter. What if Maxwell Johnson had sent him?

Silas packed up his suitcase, placed the hotel key card by the TV and left the room. The Up-arrow light on the elevator was on. Silas ran from the elevator toward the stairs in the opposite direction from his room. He stopped and hid behind the wall as someone got out of the elevator.

It was the same man, heading down the hallway in the direction of his room.

Silas scrambled down the stairs, flying past the counter. The woman at the front desk spoke to him, but he didn't stop to hear her. He got to his car, threw his suitcase in the back seat, and sped out of the parking lot.

After driving a while, he stopped at a gas station and checked the car for anything suspicious. Nothing looked like a tracker, so he got on the highway and drove for another hour just to make sure no one was following him. Then he turned around and followed the GPS from Houston to Sugar Land.

Silas called Kay to tell him he was heading to the spot earlier than planned, but he didn't tell him why he had changed his plans. Kay had set him up to stay at the house of a friend who was visiting Nigeria for three months. All Silas had to do was house sit and clean the place.

On his way there, Silas stopped by a liquor store and bought three bottles of vodka, three bottles of Hennessy, and cleared out the fridge of Guinness six-packs. He also got two family meals from a Chinese restaurant.

The house he was staying in was a bungalow with a large yard of trimmed boxwood and red and yellow shrubs, the nearest house a half-field away. When he pulled into the driveway, a middle-aged Black woman with a wide-brimmed hat was sitting on the porch of the house next door. It didn't take long before she walked over and introduced herself as the sister of an important person in town.

"He told us someone was coming," she said. "But he didn't tell us you would be this fine."

Silas forced a laugh and nodded as she gave him the rundown on the neighborhood.

"No one will bother you here," his new neighbor said. "Unless you want to be bothered." She winked at him. "Just holler if you need anything. And I do mean anything." Turning on her heels, she walked back to her porch, swaying her hips like she was strutting down an imaginary runway.

When Silas went inside the house, he stepped into a home taken straight out of an interior design magazine, with its open floor plan, curated décor and inviting white leather sectional couch. The owner was a rich young guy who split his time between Nigeria, Houston and Dubai. Everything smelled new.

The guest room was the only room with the door open. Once he dumped his things into a corner of his new space, he ventured to the clean kitchen. He planned on using it once his takeout ran out. The fridge was empty, but the pantry had three cases of bottled water, an opened bag of some strong-smelling coffee, and a few cans of chicken soup.

For the rest of the day, Silas just watched TV, alternating between chugging beers and throwing back gulps of vodka straight from the bottle. He didn't know when he passed out.

The next morning, Silas opened his eyes to find the blinding sunlight peeking through the curtains. He had fallen asleep on the couch. His head throbbed as the living room spun like a rave. The Guinness bottles were scattered on the living room floor by the brown coffee table. He yawned and gagged as vomit shot up his throat. He shouldn't have downed his liquor so fast.

Stumbling to the window, he tugged the curtains close to block out the light. He heard his phone vibrating but couldn't find it. He gave up searching for it and took a cold shower and changed his musty clothes.

He heard his phone again as he stepped out of his room. Found it in the trashcan. Missed calls from Kay, Ejiro, a dozen others, mostly women, even his dad called him. When he first left law for acting, his law professor and respected attorney Dad could never accept why Silas would abandon his thriving career for such an unserious one. Dad always expected him to go into politics and had been laying the path for years to no avail.

Silas put on the coffee maker. Kay had texted him a link to their church's website, in hopes that Silas would stream the service. Church was the last thing on his mind, though. Instead, he tapped the Glam Naija app and cursed at the headline that popped up. Top of the page, his own headshot smiled at him beside a blurry picture of Jeanie Johnson leaving his condo after hours.

'Golden boy Actor caught with media mogul's wife. Silas Harry reported missing.'

Silas tossed the phone on the couch. These corrupt media kept acting like Maxwell Johnson wasn't a vindictive thug who had crawled his way up from the streets. Silas had tried to stay away from the dirty producer, but after years of taking on supporting roles, Johnson had offered him a chance to headline a romantic drama, an offer he couldn't refuse. Now his squeaky-clean image had gone to hell in one night.

He couldn't stop replaying that night over and over in his head. Jeanie Johnson had showed up at his house in tears, looking wild and unnecessarily seductive with her breasts almost popping out of her tight gown. He should have sent her home right away, but she was crying, so he'd let her in. What were the chances that someone with a camera happened to be outside his house to catch him at the worst possible moment? The whole thing felt staged, as if an enemy had used his shaky relationship with Johnson to bring him down.

Silas grabbed his phone and clicked the link on Kay's message. Maybe church was what he needed right now to escape the chaos after all.

He caught the livestream in the middle of a man talking. He got his laptop from his suitcase to cast the service to the TV. Silas only listened to the man for a minute before almost ending the stream. Some Christians talked as if they had all the answers, but when life slapped them in the face, they acted the same way as everyone else and forgot all those nice-sounding prayers they'd prayed. That was why he hated talking to his dad.

The phone rang, Ejiro's name flashing on top of the live stream.

"I called many times," Ejiro said on the line. "Did you go to England?"

Only Kay and his wife Barbara knew that Silas was in Houston. He couldn't take the chance in case Ejiro buckled under the media pressure. But now, someone else knew he was in Houston: the man from the hotel who'd showed up at the airport waiting for him.

"You shouldn't be hiding," Ejiro continued.

"That's easy for you to say." Silas inhaled the strong coffee and took a sip. Bitter and flavorful, the real deal. "I just need a break. If they don't stop spreading lies, I'll sue for defamation."

"You not being here makes you look guilty," Ejiro countered.

"How? Did I sleep with his wife? Didn't I try to explain everything to the old goat?"

Ejiro sighed. "Do you need me to wire some money from your account?"

"I'm okay." He'd transferred fifty thousand into his dollar account the other day. "Please tell the accountant to keep sending the monthlies to my charities."

"Even now you're still thinking about charity? You want to keep acting like Naija Batman. Are all those NGO's coming forward to defend you?"

Silas put down the unfinished coffee and slumped onto the couch as he imagined Johnson foaming at the mouth to ruin his career. Johnson once mentioned that Silas might not be good for the agency brand because he didn't have any meat to attract the media vultures. Since he hadn't seriously dated in years, most of the juicy media outlets found him boring. Was it any wonder that Johnson had finally pounced on the chance to get rid of him? No one would hold it against the man, especially since Silas had gone viral for being the homewrecker who seduced another man's wife.

"Sorry," Ejiro went on. "I'm doing what I can, but it won't mean anything if you don't come back soon. The reporter you beat up has filed a lawsuit. He's saying it's assault."

"How can he even claim that?" Silas growled. "He was in my freaking house looking for God knows what."

"That's not the story he's telling."

Silas took a deep breath, stilling as he heard music from his laptop. A small orchestra played an instrumental, a hymn he recognized from the days when he was determined to make time for church. But this version of the hymn was different, a modern rendition that could be played in a jazz lounge.

He turned up the volume as the melody changed and a soulful voice exploded from the stage. The camera zoomed onto one of the four people standing in front of the instrumentalists--a cocoa brown Black woman as beautiful as her smoky voice with thick hair flying around her like a wild mane.

"My hands are holding you..." she sang, dancing around the stage. She broke into a half-run before stopping so suddenly like she had strings attached to her. The other singers around her kept moving in that boring church singer's way, pumping their fists and lifting their hands to heaven in some weird trance as if to convince people they were seeing the Spirit no one else could.

Silas sat down on the carpet in front of the laptop, tensing as he watched the strange woman drop to her knees and place her forehead on the floor. After a moment, she jumped to her feet, and her voice got louder and more soulful. The whole performance was nuts. The chick wasn't even wearing shoes. She danced from one end of the stage to the other and the stage light fell on her like a thick glow fanning out around her. The camera zoomed in and she opened her eyes to offer a breathtaking smile before she picked up a guitar and started playing.

"Thank God," she whispered in a quiet voice.

He couldn't tear his eyes away from her. She was unlike any other woman he ever met, and it wasn't just because she was beautiful. Everything about her screamed...he couldn't quite find the word he was looking for.

"Silas," a voice shouted. "Are you okay?"

He snapped his attention back to the forgotten phone in his hand. "Yeah, I heard you." How long had Ejiro been talking?

"Who's that singing?"

"Some chick." He could find out from Kay. No, Silas shook his head. He was supposed to be laying low, and a woman like that would only draw attention. He snuck in one last look at her and slammed his laptop shut.

"She's no one," Silas murmured. He opened the fridge to grab another bottle of vodka.

2

"My hands are holding you," Ibelema hummed, jogging down the stairs with her guitar, late for choir practice at church.

"You look nice," Mom said, with a cryptic smile, sitting at the dining table with Dad drinking herbal tea. Dad started a fast at the beginning of the year because he had an urgent request, and apparently, God listened better to people who were fasting.

Ibelema twirled around in her *ankara*-printed jumpsuit. Dad grunted, meaning he approved. Ever since Kenneth dumped her—played was a better word—Dad was more vocal about what she wore to church. "Don't give these people anything more to talk about," he once said to her, and never brought up the matter again. Message received.

"Do you want to grab something to go?" Mom asked.

"They'll feed us," Ibelema replied. "I need to get on the road now."

Caught in the Spirit, Deacon Dad paid her no mind. He

gestured for her to sit down and launched into a solemn praise session as if he was in front of his Sunday school class. Mom hummed along until she interrupted Dad's song to pray for direction for Ibelema's life, motioning for Ibelema to kneel.

The prayer kept going and going. Ibelema's neck hurt from holding still under Mom's firm hand. These days, their prayers sounded desperate. They were worried about her future, and instead of bringing peace, the prayers seemed to make them more anxious.

"I had a dream," Mom announced, once she was done praying.

Ibelema managed to smile. She didn't have time today for Mom's vague prophetic dreams. The true miracle was that Dad hadn't asked about her job search.

Mom's eyes sparkled with tears, and maybe excitement? "Yesterday, as I was praying, it came to me. This month, you're going to meet your husband. I saw a man I've never seen. He came here with his mother, and the funny thing is I know her from somewhere, but couldn't place her in the dream —"

"She's already late," Dad said in a tight voice, clearly tired of Mom's dreams concerning Ibelema's kingdom spouse.

"Can't I talk to my daughter?" Mom countered with steely eyes.

Dad got up. "Have you forgotten what happened the last time?" Shaking his head, he left the dining room without waiting for a response. Mom's last revelation of Ibelema's future husband had ended in the supposed "husband" asking someone else to marry him.

Ibelema said goodbye and rushed out of the house. Dad would get an earful from Mom, but she couldn't blame either of them. How could she get upset at her parents when her prayers were just as desperate? For the most part, she'd done everything they wanted, including getting the Nursing degree which had only added a mountain to her student loans. Who knew it would be this hard finding a nursing position? A year after graduation, Ibelema had only rejection letters to show for a lifetime of diligent study. Everyone said that once she finished school, she would have well-paying jobs lined up for her to choose from. Instead, she was stuck working at her Aunty Osagie's home health company.

But after months of languishing away, Ibelema was finally doing what she always wanted to do. Working on her film had given her new life in a way she never expected. The problem now was she had run out of time to find someone to play the Reverend.

When Ibelema got to church, the media team was done setting up and the worship team was on stage for the sound check. As she crossed the aisle toward the stage, Efe met her half-way.

"Love that jumpsuit," Efe cooed. "Lemme hold it for this thing I have next week."

"Sure." Ibelema laughed. Efe was the little sister she never had, so they always borrowed each other's clothes. "I thought you had class this evening."

Efe wrinkled her nose. "Why is Skinny coming this way?" Only a few people could twist Efe's face like that.

Skinny Ruth stopped in front of the pew. "IB," Ruth called, with her all-too-bright smile. She didn't look Efe's way. "You didn't respond to the invitation. My friend said she sent it to you."

Ibelema felt her face tingle. "What invitation?" Was this woman seriously expecting her to come? She might as well have slapped her.

Ruth pouted. "My bridal shower, you didn't get it?"

Normal people would correctly assume that Ibelema's silence meant she didn't want to go to her ex-boyfriend's fiancée's bridal shower, but ever since Ruth found out that her fiancé Kenneth had thought of marrying Ibelema, she'd gone out of her way to make every interaction between them extremely uncomfortable.

"You probably didn't recognize the sender," Ruth pressed.

"Maybe it's in her junk folder," Efe said with a fake smile. "Since it's spam."

Ruth eyed Efe and Ibelema nudged her friend's arm. "I'll check again," Ibelema said.

"It's next month. We would love for you to be there." Ruth's smile faded when Efe made a disgruntled sound. She looked Efe up and down before walking to the front.

Efe let out a long hiss. "What a ridiculous human being. I'll never understand how he could pick her over you. And I hope you're not actually thinking about going to her shower."

Ibelema walked toward the stage. "It's the right thing to do."

"God, IB, why do you always have to be this way?"

"What way is that?"

"For once just be dramatic." Efe rolled her eyes. "Either way, she sucks, and God help their children 'cause they're both trash."

"That's not nice." Kenneth once talked about how he wanted his first child to be a boy. He wanted two boys and two girls, and Ibelema had simply laughed at him because she thought it was a nice dream and didn't know what else to say. She'd never been the sort to sweet talk a guy and say things she didn't mean, but when she started dating Kenneth, she'd started to imagine having children with a man for the first time in her life.

"I don't understand her," Efe said. "She stole the guy, so why must she keep rubbing it in your face?"

The piano boomed across the auditorium, interrupting Efe's tirade. Ibelema handed Efe her purse and rushed to the stage with her guitar. There, several associate pastors and others were huddled by the front pews. Ruth snuggled against Kenneth, who looked at Ibelema with the same apologetic smile she'd come to ignore. She walked past them up the side stairs and stood with Pastor Luke on stage.

As usual, time flew and practice ran late, but Ibelema never complained about worship team duties. Since they named her high school worship leader three years ago, she'd thought it was only a matter of months before Pastor Luke made her a permanent member of the worship team. Hopefully, it would finally happen, and Dad would get off her back about what she was doing with her life.

When practice ended, Ibelema drove home. She looked over some video footage and approved changes to a revised scene Daniel had sent over. Before going to bed, she grabbed her guitar and fiddled with a song she was working on. Then she sang her mind to sleep.

The next morning, Ibelema checked in at her job and ran errands for Aunt Osagie. She had promised to meet Kimani and Daniel after she clocked out, but didn't get to the plaza until evening. Daniel's gray Honda and Kimani's snazzy Rav4 were the only cars parked in front of the suite, meaning the lovebirds Tari and Judah had left the office.

At the front double doors, she heard the buzz that unlocked the door, and she went inside the building. The side door attaching Tari's office to the lobby was closed. For the past year, the Vessels Fellowship had held its meetings in the main room which could seat over a hundred people. Apart from Tari's office in the front, there were two smaller offices in the back, and a kitchen area with a sink and stove. The former owner had retired to Tanzania and was renting the place to Judah for peanuts with an option to buy—all thanks to Papa Teka, who had put the deal together.

It was a peace-filling place. Ibelema liked coming here for the meetings, but loved it more when the hall was empty. The waves of calm flowed into her soul and made her want to burst into song. Last week, Phoebe had said the same thing when they met up here with Kimani and Eden to discuss wedding plans. Kimani and Tari were tasked with helping organize the wedding, while Ibelema, Eden, Efe and others were ushers for the ceremony and reception. It was nice of Phoebe to want to honor Papa and Mama Teka by getting married at their church.

"You're late," Kimani called from the back.

When Ibelema entered the room, Kimani hugged her tightly. They met four years ago when Kimani started attending her church and had been cool ever since. Although Ibelema knew Barbara from high school, Kimani was her closest friend as they gelled better because of their no-drama approach to life.

Daniel looked up from the two screens on his desk to the other huge flat screen hanging on the wall. He and Judah used this room and the one next door for trading the stock market. Tari said they were great at it and were now looking to invest other people's money, which Ibelema unfortunately had none of.

"Any luck with the location for Scene 5?" Daniel asked, a half-eaten sandwich and a cup of coffee on his desk.

Ibelema dropped on an empty seat. "United, Mama's Kitchen

all said no. Even Finger—"

"It doesn't fit your aesthetic," he said, never taking his eyes from his computer.

"You're starting to sound like me." He was always messing with her, right from the day Kimani first introduced them. Kimani had known Judah and Daniel since college, but Ibelema only met Daniel two years ago, and sometimes she wondered why she was so comfortable with him already. She had known Kenneth since middle school and never felt free around Kenneth. But that wasn't Kenneth's fault. Daniel had this weird superpower of making people feel immediately comfortable around him. She'd seen it at work many times. It was probably one of the things that made him such a great writer.

"Did you try that suya restaurant off Kirkwood?" Kimani asked, eyes fixed on her phone.

"All that won't matter if I can't find someone to play the Reverend," Ibelema moaned.

"What about Kay's friend who's supposed to be in town?" Daniel asked.

"That's a last resort."

Daniel took a sip of his coffee. "He's an actor. Plus, Kay said he'd be the perfect Reverend. Have you looked him up?"

Ibelema never liked the idea of Googling people. "It's complicated." Anyways, the guy didn't even show up to Kay's wedding. What sort of best friend was that?

"And the Rev's daughter?" Daniel asked. "Is that still complicated too?"

Last week, the youth pastor had asked Ibelema to join their meeting about Chanel, a girl accused of sowing division in the student ministry. Ultimately, the pastor had asked Chanel not to attend their student gatherings for a while, and he set up private meetings to help Chanel "understand the error of her ways." The most ridiculous part of the meeting was when the leaders urged Ibelema to consider removing Chanel from her film, which was partly sponsored by the church. As the high school worship leader, Ibelema had known Chanel since the girl was in middle school, and casting Chanel as the Reverend's daughter was a no-brainer.

"Chanel is my baby," Ibelema said. Yet she was in a tough place. If she didn't listen to the youth pastor about Chanel, he might complain about her to Pastor Luke, which would endanger her hopes for a permanent staff position on the main worship team—a position she'd been praying for long before she went to nursing school. If Ibelema could get a paying position on the team, then she could pursue making films without having to bother about getting another job.

"Christians can be so full of crap," Kimani quipped. "If they're trying to kick her out of the ministry, what does that have to do with you?"

From what Ibelema heard, some high school girls didn't like Chanel because she kept to herself, so they snitched on her after the golden boy of their ministry had confessed to his small group that he slept with Chanel after she flirted with him. Instead of putting their arms around Chanel, the girls ostracized her. Why couldn't the leaders understand it was mostly jealousy? Besides, Chanel was far from the first person at church to have sex before marriage.

"Does anyone believe that soft gentle Chanel actually seduced him?" Kimani spat.

"Yeah, right." Ibelema got up from the chair and started

pacing the room. "That boy is so fake yet he acts like he's so spiritual and can do no wrong. She's clearly the victim, but church politics, you know. The dude's dad is one of the heavy hitters at church. Gives a lot of money."

Kimani smiled wryly, making a gesture with her palms smoothing her chest to tell Ibelema to calm down.

"You breathe too," Ibelema teased.

Kimani laughed. "We know it's serious if Miss-I-don't-like-drama is getting involved," she said to Daniel before giving Ibelema a squeeze. "Anyways, I have to go get Thandi. We'll catch up. Thanks, D." She rushed out of the place like someone was chasing her. The one thing Kimani never played with was her daughter, Thandi.

"Did you review the changes?" Daniel asked when they were alone.

Her phone buzzed with a message from Mom asking her to come home early today. "Sorry, I gotta go too. But yeah, your draft changes are gold." A smile spread across her lips. "I really appreciate you looking out for me. Do you know I plan to name my first son after you?"

Daniel chuckled. "You'll have to nab Mr. IB first."

"Oh, Mr. IB, where are you?" she said, with dramatic flair.

"Please find the Reverend first."

"I'm working on that." The wrap deadline was a month away and they still hadn't filmed the most important scenes. Since the Rev only appeared in a few shots, Ibelema had saved his scenes for last.

Ibelema waited for Daniel to say something encouraging. He understood more than anyone how hope deferred could make a heart grow sick.

"I didn't even ask how your day went," she said after a moment.

Daniel shrugged. "Won a trade, everything this week will go to the edit. Efe said she's got two pros we could check out."

"I can't take any more money from you. We'll find cheaper editors."

"We can't compromise on quality just because of money."

She released her breath. "But—"

"Just check out the Kirkwood location first. It'll work itself out."

Nodding, Ibelema waved bye to him before heading to the doors. Once outside, she heard someone call her name. She turned and saw a face she recognized, barely managing to cringe as a beaming man strolled over. She couldn't quite remember his name or where she first met him, but Ibelema kept running into this same guy year after year, and at the most random times.

"I knew that was your car," the man said, shoving his hands in his pockets. He ogled her openly before letting out a low whistle. "God, you're looking finer than ever."

Ibelema didn't try to smile. "Thanks. I'm in a hurry." She opened the driver's side door of her car, but he put his hand on the door to block her.

"Can't a brotha get a minute?"

"I'm late for a meeting," she said.

"Then give me your number."

"Sorry, I can't." Nigerian guys could be so full of themselves for no reason at all.

He grabbed her hand. "I still don't see no ring."

Ibelema snatched her hand back from him. "I really have to go." She started to enter her car, but he grabbed her arm again.

"What's this place?" He looked back at the suite. "My guy owns the shop over there. Said he sees all kinds of people around here, but it ain't got no sign."

"It's like a fellowship." Ibelema yanked her hand away and ducked into her car. "Take care."

He got in the way of her closing the door. "See, that's why you're still not married. You need to learn how to treat a man."

"What?" She didn't even know him, so why did he think he could come at her?

"You're always acting like you're better than everyone and yet you still can't find a man," he spat, the meanness of his words emphasizing the scowl on his face. "What you need to do is come down your high horse and give a brotha a chance."

Ibelema jerked the door toward her, but he let go before his fingers caught in the closed door.

"You crazy—"

"What's going on here?" Daniel's voice sounded out of nowhere. He marched toward her car, his brows furrowed and his jaw set in a way that Ibelema knew he was mad. This must be the side of him that Kimani had told her a little about Daniel and Judah's past where they used to be wild boys selling drugs.

Ibelema jumped out of the car to stand in between Daniel and the pest. Daniel was already having enough problems with his immigration status, and getting him into any trouble was the last thing she wanted.

"I'm sorry," Ibelema said to the fool through a forced smile. "It was a mistake. I didn't mean to disrespect you."

The man looked at her in confusion, then at Daniel's hard face. "It's cool," he said, backing away towards the store he claimed his friend owned.

Daniel watched him go until Ibelema snapped her fingers. "It's all good. Just leave it." She entered her car again.

"What was that about?" Daniel called.

Ibelema didn't let him reach the car, starting the engine before he could launch into a lecture. "Love you, bro. Thanks for always looking out."

He didn't smile. "Anytime, but—"

Ibelema blinked away a tear and drove out of the parking lot before the fake smile melted away from her face.

3

After spending three days indoors without going anywhere, Silas finally left the house to meet up with Kay and Barbara. He'd told Kay what happened at the hotel and why he couldn't visit them, but Barbara still insisted that he come see them, just somewhere else. She picked a restaurant in Sugar Land that served good suya. When Silas googled the place, a handful of reviews claimed that it was the perfect space for patrons looking for privacy. "Hardly anyone there when we visit," one reviewer wrote.

On his way to the restaurant, Silas got lost a couple of times, but when he finally found the place, the parking lot was empty, as Barbara had promised. A plate of hot suya and a cold drink would do him good.

Inside, the restaurant was clean with a cozy feel, smothered by the smell of grilled meat and spices. Photos of African landmarks lined the yellow walls. On the wall facing the door, a handwritten menu on a blackboard behind the counter displayed the varieties of suya, coconut and jollof rice with fried plantain, different soups and starches.

When the door under the blackboard menu opened, Silas lowered his baseball cap over his eyes. A scrawny older man stepped out like he was surprised to see someone there.

"To go or for here?" he asked, from behind the counter.

"For here," Silas said. "I'm expecting two others." Kay had texted that they were running late. "But let me start with three beef suya and three shrimp suya while I wait." He sat near the door, the one way in and out.

Minutes later, the man set a plate of grilled beef and shrimp on the table. The meat looked rubbery, overcooked, clearly not like the suya back home. And where were the condiments?

Picking at the tough meat stuck in his teeth, Silas pulled up a Nigerian news app on his phone. Each new story was worse, labeling him a charlatan who also sucked at acting. On top of everything, all his hard work as an actor was for nothing. The news was spreading like wildfire online. It was only a matter of time before every Nigerian in Houston knew his name and face.

The front door swung open, and a woman entered the restaurant. Silas faced the wall, pretending to be busy on his phone so she wouldn't see him. But when she stopped at the counter, she glanced at him, and he peered at her from the corner of his eye. Voluminous afro, *ankara* print jumpsuit, and colorful sneakers. The way the jumpsuit hugged her slim shapely figure made him sneak more peeks at her. God, she was wicked gorgeous. As if he didn't already have enough on his plate, the devil had sent him a new temptation.

The woman tapped the counter, waiting for someone to show up.

"He's back there," Silas said out of nowhere, mentally slapping himself for opening his mouth. But he'd talked to her so she would turn around again, and she did. Her dark eyes looked him over, and the eye contact unnerved him to the point that he got up so suddenly his chair fell back against the wall before crashing down.

Silas picked up the chair and sat down again, a realization dawning on him. It was her, the woman from the church service. Had Kay told her to come? But he never said anything to Kay about her.

She strolled to his table with the sort of smile that made a man forget himself. "Say something," she said, in this low, sexy voice.

"What?"

"Anything. Just say something."

Did she recognize him and wanted to make sure he was Silas Harry? "I think you have the wrong person."

"You have a nice voice," she almost sang, then seemed to notice his confusion. "Sorry, that sounds super weird."

His heart was racing. Women hit on him all the time and he reminded himself this wasn't any different. But whoever she was, she was different. She was the woman who had stirred his soul just days ago.

The vision in *ankara* made herself comfortable in the chair opposite from him. "Do you come here often?"

It was so cheesy, but coming from her, it sounded like the best pickup line. Her bright eyes swept over his face, prompting Silas to scoot back again, his chair loudly scraping the floor. She definitely knew him... or had Kay told her to meet them here?

"Sorry," she said. "It looks like I'm freaking you out."

He held up his thumb against his forefinger. "A little."

She chuckled. "Well, you can rest easy, I'm not trying to hit on you or anything like that." Silas raised a brow, and she suddenly looked scandalized. "Is that what you think I'm doing?"

He shook his head, not knowing what to think now. It wasn't like he minded the idea of her hitting on him. Her voice echoed in his head like a song waiting to be sung, and she was looking at him now like she didn't care who he was, not at all awed by him. She just... saw him.

"Whatever," she said. "Meeting you here like this has to be God."

Silas tried not to laugh. "Why is that?"

She pressed her sweet, full lips together. "I need your help. Have you ever been in a movie?"

"A movie?" He knew his share of overzealous fans, but none of them—not even crazy Jeanie Johnson—could compare to this woman. Had the devil sent her to finish him here? He scanned the café before looking back at her sparkling eyes. The server still hadn't come to check on the new customer.

"I'm making a movie and think you'd be perfect for one of my characters," she said. "If you help me, I promise I'll make it worth your while."

Before she finished talking, the front door opened. "Sorry we're late," Kay said. "Tiwa's grandma didn't get to the house on time." A smiling woman elbowed Kay to the side. Silas instantly recognized her, even though they had only seen each other on video calls.

"Look at how she just pushed her husband," Kay said.

Silas nudged Kay out of his way. "Please, move so I can greet my sister."

"I know why I always liked you," Barbara said, laughing. "And now finally I get to meet you. Welcome to Houston." She leaned in and stopped. "Can I hug you?" She flung her arms around him. "I'm so happy you're here."

Silas hugged her back. "Sorry it took me so long to get here."

"Don't apologize," she said, letting go of him. "You were busy and life happened. We're just glad you agreed to come." Barbara looked past Silas. "I see you've met IB."

Silas felt like someone had poured hot tea over him. The beautiful woman was the famous IB who could do no wrong? He turned and met her widened stare. She looked way different from the dolled-up maid of honor at Kay's wedding years ago.

"You're...Tonye?" she squeaked, like a completely different woman, almost as if he imagined all that flirtatious energy from earlier.

"My mans for life," Kay said, putting his arm around Silas.

Silas glared at his friend. Kay had always called him Tonye, simply because Kay knew how much he hated his name. When Silas first went into acting, his manager Ejiro had suggested that he use his middle name instead of his given first name. Silas Harry just sounded more legit.

Silas reached out to shake her hand. "It's nice to finally meet you." For years, he'd heard all about Barbara's amazing friend who turned heads yet was so spiritual that she refused to date anyone. As far as he knew, if he'd made it to the wedding, the couple would have hooked them up. Was that why Kay invited her here? What were the chances of IB being the same woman from the church service?

She seemed to hesitate before taking his hand. "Yeah." Her dark eyes studied his face and he must have held on too long because she tugged her hand away.

"What were you guys talking about when we walked in?" Kay asked, looking between them.

"You were saying you would make it worth his while," Barbara teased, wiggling her brows at an embarrassed IB who covered her face. "He just got here and you're already ambushing him."

"It's cool." Silas shot Kay a grin. He would have dabbed him up if the women weren't there. Barbara wanted to hook him up with this beauty? And she made movies too?

"Yeah, it's nothing." IB didn't look at him.

"She just asked me to be in her movie," Silas said.

"You already asked him to be the Rev?" Kay asked.

"Welcome sir. Are you ready to order?" The man stood behind the counter watching them. Silas shot him a withering look. Why did it take him so long to show up?

IB checked her phone. "Actually, I have somewhere to be. Can we talk to the owner now about shooting here?"

Kay smiled at her. "Don't worry. Just go. I got this."

"You're sure?"

"Yeah, I'll get him to say yes."

"Thanks, bro." She looked at Silas and her tone changed.

"Welcome to Houston, Kay's friend. Hope you enjoy your stay."

Kay's friend? Why was she acting stiff toward him all of a sudden? Silas waited for IB to talk more about her movie, but she linked arms with Barbara, acting as if she wanted nothing else to do with him.

"Go ahead and order," Barbara called over her shoulder, as the pair bounced out of the restaurant glued to each other's side.

Silas watched them leave and followed Kay to the counter, where they placed their order before going back to the table.

"Why did you tell her my name is Tonye?"

"Isn't that your name?" Kay asked, with a naughty smile. "It's IB," he added, as if it answered the question.

"She's really something," Silas said, trying to downplay his interest.

"That's why you should be in her movie," Kay said.

Didn't Kay understand the trouble he was in? "I'm supposed to be laying low."

"Trust me, this is your best way forward." Kay laughed and stood. "You just have to play along. IB could be the best thing that ever happened to you."

The glint in his eyes made Silas glance back at the front door. At this point, what more did he have to lose by playing along? Now that he'd finally met her, he understood why Kay and Barbara thought IB would be good for him. She was like a burning ray of light that could pierce through any darkness. He had maybe three more months in Houston, and IB would certainly make the time worth his while. His heart started beating faster just thinking about the way she said the words. He almost shivered.

"Are you with me?" Kay asked.

"Always," Silas said, smiling as he followed Kay outside.

4

"What's his deal?" Ibelema asked, once they were outside the restaurant. Why did the guy seem so anxious?

Barbara gave a look like she didn't want to talk about it. Both husband and wife were strangely quiet about Kay's best friend's visit. She couldn't believe they asked her to meet them at the restaurant and didn't tell her Tonye would be there.

"You're the one who pounced on him," Barbara pointed out. "Cut him some slack."

Pounced was a little too much. "Why are you guys being so secretive about his visit? Is there another reason he's here?"

"He's Tiwa's godfather. Does he need another reason to come here?"

Ibelema held her hands up in surrender. "No need for the scary eyes." The two of them had been friends since middle school youth group at church, and when Barbara got married, Kay talked about setting her up with his best friend. Kay had wanted him to be the best man, but Tonye couldn't make time to travel. Just how busy was he to miss his best friend's wedding? Or was he just a jerk? Kay was too nice to have a jerk for a best friend.

"Sorry," Barbara said, with a sigh. "I know he seemed weird, but he's really a good guy. One of the best. You'll see."

"Sure. He does have a nice voice though." The second Tonye opened his mouth was a revelation. He sounded exactly how Ibelema imagined the Reverend would when she wrote the character.

"And?" Barbara prodded.

"And nothing."

"This girl. Sometimes, you don't have any sense. You were just talking to him like that?"

"How was I talking to him?"

Barbara licked her lips. "I promise to make it worth your while," she said, with a spicy impression of Ibelema's voice.

"That's not how I sounded," Ibelema protested before looking back at the restaurant. Was that how Tonye had taken it? If so, she had to leave now. What was she thinking saying that to him?

"You understand now, huh?" Barbara started laughing hysterically. "You were probably just going in and didn't even see he was looking at you like he might eat you whole instead of the suya he ordered."

"Jesus, Barb. You and your mouth." Ibelema muffled her laugh. "How did you guys even hear me all the way from outside?"

The door opened suddenly, and the two men stepped out. "What's so funny?" Kay asked.

"Nothing," Ibelema quickly replied, making a face at Barbara, who was doing a bad job of controlling her mirth. She smacked Barbara's hand. How could she look at Tonye now?

"Why didn't you tell me you were trying to use this place for a scene?" Kay asked.

Ibelema shrugged. "I didn't think about it until Daniel mentioned it."

Kay snapped his fingers. "For Scene 5, right? Let's do it. I know the owner; he'll love the attention."

"Is there anyone you don't know?" Barbara asked.

"Are you the one talking, Madame Houston?" Kay fired back playfully. Between Kay and Barbara, they knew at least half of the Nigerians in Houston.

Ibelema stuck out her tongue at Barbara, but caught Tonye staring at her and closed her mouth.

"We were just talking about your film actually," Kay continued. "Tonye would definitely be good as the Rev."

Ibelema glanced at Tonye. Good wasn't the word. More like perfection, with his striking face, surgical jaw. Dressed casual in black jeans and a loose t-shirt, his stone muscles strained against the fabric and made her look away. Ibelema couldn't work with him. He gave off the arrogant vibe of a man who had convinced himself that he was God's gift to women.

"They didn't tell me you're a writer," Tonye said.

Why was he licking his lips? Who did he think he was, LL Cool J?

"IB's working on her first movie for TIFF this year," Barbara chimed in with a proud smile.

Tonye looked impressed. "What's it about?"

Ibelema realized she was clenching her fist. Instead of trying to convince the guy who could solve her problem, she was judging him unfairly. The chance that Kay's unreliable best friend just happened to be the exact man she was looking for could only mean that God had brought him here at the perfect time.

"It's about a man searching for himself," Ibelema replied. She'd talked about the film so many times that she could describe scene-by-scene half asleep. But Tonye had experience in acting, so what he probably needed to know was the essence of the script, not a drawn-out explanation.

"After a scandal," she went on, "he starts to lose faith in everything he's known, and has to confront the hypocrisy of his world, embodied by the Reverend---the mentor he no longer believes in."

Tonye pushed his glasses up the bridge of his nose. "A Christian film?" His eyes seemed to mock her.

"What's wrong with a Christian film?" Barbara asked, raising a brow.

"Nothing," Tonye said. "I just—" Kay bumped his shoulder to silence him.

"It's a movie analyzing Christian culture," Ibelema explained. "Most Christians will probably hate it."

"And why's that?"

"It highlights the corruption of church politics, greed, betrayal, even some danger. It's a drama thriller, so not quite the cheesy films you might be thinking of."

"So...it's a church project?"

Ibelema forced a smile. He clearly thought it wasn't worth his time. And why would he? Even her own family didn't believe in her filmmaking. "Some church members contributed money, but it's mostly crowd-funded."

Tonye nodded. "Good for you."

Ibelema held his gaze. While she spoke, she noticed Tonye's look change from curiosity to condescension, as if he'd concluded the whole thing was beneath him. But now his eyes hinted that he was interested again. In the film or her? Either way, Ibelema knew that look. She knew guys like him in college and had made it a point to stay far away from them. Barbara was right—Tonye was a bad boy. If she gave him an inch, he would take more than she was willing to give. It would be silly trying to cast someone like him in her God-inspired movie.

"It's perfectly fine if you don't want to," she said.

"I thought you said he was the perfect fit," Barbara jumped in.

Tonye smiled. "Maybe she isn't that confident in her script after all."

"She is," Kay countered. "It's good stuff."

Ibelema nearly laughed. Tonye was baiting her, trying to reel her in. If he was interested in her, she should use that against him. She didn't have time to find another Reverend. And wasn't this a sign? If Tonye wasn't meant to play the Rev, why was he such an obvious choice?

"At least read the script," Kay pressed his friend with a nudge.

Barbara clapped her hands. "If you do, you'll be dying to play the part."

Tonye tapped his lips like he was thinking about it. "Send me the script then. What's your number? I'll call you when I'm done looking it over."

Did he really think it was going to be that easy? "You can let Kay know what you think," Ibelema agreed. "This Friday, we're filming a scene in the Y. If and when you're ready, you can come there to audition for—"

"Audition?" He looked shocked and offended, making Kay and Barbara chuckle. "For what? You're practically begging me to play the hero."

Tonye's arrogance was on point for the Rev. "Look, if you want to be in my film, you have to audition, just to be sure we're on the same page."

He rubbed his jaw, looking her over once more with that chilling bad-boy stare. This time Ibelema looked away first. "Cool," Tonye said. "I still have to like the script, so I guess we'll see."

"Friday, 6pm. Kay will send you the address." Tonye seemed like a man used to getting whatever he wanted, but his smugness needed to be taken down a notch.

"By the way," Ibelema added. "You're the Reverend, not the hero." He looked confused. "You'll understand when you read the script." She pointed at the door as the owner came out of the restaurant waving them down. "I think your food is ready."

Tonye offered her a charming grin before going back into the restaurant, and Ibelema exhaled deeply once the door shut behind him.

Kay patted her back. "I'll talk to the owner."

One more step closer to her dream. "The best decision Barb ever made was marrying you," Ibelema called to Kay, who gave her a thumbs up on his way back inside. To think she'd almost had to arm-wrestle her friend into going on that first date with the dashing lawyer.

"And I'll never forget you had a lot to do with that. Your turn is coming, IB." Kay grinned. "But please keep reminding this woman for me." He hurried in before Barbara could respond.

"What a joker," Barbara quipped, her dimples belying her irritation with her husband.

Ibelema hugged her. "I'm out," she said, heading to her car.

"We still seeing you tomorrow?" Barbara asked, and Ibelema

frowned. "You forgot? You promised to help with Tiwa's hair for our picture day."

Ibelema hesitated for a moment. "Is he going to be there?"

"Who, Tonye? No, he has a lot going on."

Ibelema wanted to ask what, but knowing any more about the man would bring her trouble. After the fiasco with Kenneth, men were the last thing on her mind. What she needed now was to finish this film, and if Tonye could help her do it, then she would tolerate him for as long as necessary, and hopefully, the man wasn't as bad as she thought.

5

Silas stayed up all night. He couldn't close his eyes without hearing her sexy voice, her dazzling eyes flashing in the silence of his room. How could one woman be so talented? IB not only sang like some dark angel, but she also wrote like a Shakespearean incarnate. Her script "A Week on the Mountain" was masterful. Once he started reading, he didn't put it down.

The drama was about a young pastor who joined a mission to start several churches in Texas. As he went about church-planting, he discovered some shady happenings with the church's finances among other issues. Set during a convention week in Houston with the Honorable Reverend, the young pastor is forced to make things right and confront the man of God whom he has lost faith in.

Pastor Samuel, the young firebrand, was a little annoying with his self-righteous attitude, but somehow, he was also a likable main character. His strong convictions were worthy of thought, the kind of hero Silas loved to play. But the Honorable Reverend Obiora stole the show, though he only appeared in a handful of scenes. IB's Rev was a domineering, suck-the-air-out-of-the-room figure who didn't care what anyone thought about him, and yet he read like a father who loved Samuel. All the Rev wanted was to hold on to the old established ways of doing ministry, but in the process, he hurt many people. The interactions between the two men were heartbreaking, every spoken word leading to the inevitable betrayal. From the moment the Rev was introduced deep into the second act, Silas found himself defending the man, even though he also understood Samuel's decision to abandon the Reverend.

When the betrayal finally happened, Silas mumbled a curse into the darkness. The Rev was the villain, but he read like an antihero, a man both relatable and memorable.

Silas lowered his phone and sat back against his bed frame, deep in thought. The Rev wasn't like any of the roles he'd auditioned for in the past. What sort of person could write characters like this? He had to play the Reverend, so he needed to work with IB. He could invest in her movie and make her so indebted him that she could write more scripts for him. Maybe this was his chance–he could step away from the limelight and start a production company with IB as his screenwriter. In time, social media would forget about him and his company's success could speak for itself. Then he could devote more time to non-profit work. He had always wanted to travel and see more areas in Africa that needed help.

His phone rang, shaking him out of his daydream. Dad. Silas wasn't ready to talk yet. He hid the phone under the pillows and went to the kitchen to warm some chicken soup.

When he came back to the room, the sun was up, light

filtering through the curtains. He sent Kay a text, and his best friend called minutes later.

"Who the heck is this chick? This script is wild."

Kay laughed. "Told you. How far have you gotten?"

"I'm done." No point in beating around the bush. Kay was right. IB could be the best thing for him. "If she's writing like this, who knows what else she can write for me?"

"She has a mountain of material. And wait till you meet this other guy, Daniel. He might be even be better than IB is. He's working on this ridiculous novel about his past that reads like an Aaron Sorkin/Spike Lee screenplay."

Silas made some coffee while Kay waxed poetic about this Daniel's work. Kay had a sense for talent and always had a hunch about what movie scripts would do well at the box office. After Silas' first successful gig, Kay pleaded with his friend to refuse the next two roles he auditioned for because their scripts were "missing that spark." Both movies had bombed.

"It's not the typical role I'd go for," Silas admitted.

Kay sucked his teeth. "Romcoms are child's play for you, man. You were always meant for heavier, more complex stuff."

The coffee maker sounded like little balloons popping. "I get the feeling she has beef with me."

"This is going to be fun." Kay chuckled, not denying Silas' guess. "But on a serious note, you do have to tell her about the stuff back home."

Silas grabbed a mug from the dishwasher. "She doesn't know?"

"No. Why would I tell her?"

"But she knows I'm an actor. She's probably going to Google me now and find out."

"I doubt it. IB's weird with social media. It's better if you tell her yourself, and soon. She's got a serious issue with people lying."

Silas filled his cup with coffee. The woman didn't seem like anything could disturb her unflappable personality. "Bad experience with a guy?"

"Yeah." Kay said, not bothering to share more. Before long, he said he needed to feed Tiwa but would send the address for Friday. He snickered saying the word "audition," then hung up.

Silas was wide awake, though he hadn't slept last night. He opened his laptop, thinking of her. IB. He didn't know her full name, but clicked to YouTube, looked up her church's channel, and selected one of the worship videos. She wasn't part of the music ministry that day, so he scoured other videos before he found her. IB didn't dance around as much in this one, just played her guitar and sang in that smoky voice. Smoky was the only word he could think of to describe her Lauryn Hill vibe. Her stage presence was off the charts, and with the easy way she played around with her guitar, it was hard to believe that being a singer wasn't her main talent. She seemed like the sort of woman who could do anything she wanted, and always got what she wanted when she wanted, the kind who didn't quit when she put her mind to something, and would rally everyone to her cause in such a way that they would start believing it was their idea in the first place. IB was the most dangerous type of woman—one who didn't realize the power she held over people.

An hour later, Silas was about to watch his fourth worship video when it struck him that he should stop. He was spiraling. If he was going to get IB to help his career, he needed to be in control of his feelings. He had to make her want him, need him, not the other way around. If he fell for her this early, he would lose his edge. Whoever fell in love first lost the power in the dynamic. Slam-dunking IB's audition would give him one foot in, then he could learn more about what made her tick.

Against his better judgment, Silas let the playlist continue, and the next YouTube video was a worship session for high school kids. IB sat on the stage with her legs crossed, no shoes on, and sang her heart out, half-crying, half-laughing. The whole video was strange. He thought to skip to the next one, but couldn't bear to miss a moment of her. Yet by the end of the video, he caught a tear rolling down his face, and another followed. Was it the scandal that had made him more emotional? He slammed the laptop and climbed into bed.

Under the covers, Silas closed his eyes and her words flowed through him like the river of life she sang about. "When's the last time you really talked to God?" she'd asked as she softly strummed her guitar.

He couldn't remember. How did he survive the past weeks without praying? There was a time when God meant a lot to him, but like IB's song, he'd drifted his own way and left God standing there. He always told himself that his problem wasn't with God. The real issue was the world, the injustice and cruelty, the abandoned children, bad people who forged ahead while good ones starved and died waiting for a miracle. But if God truly existed, how could God allow so much evil?

Silas' eyes blinked open, and tears poured out before he could stop them. "I'm sorry," he said, not sure if he was talking to himself or praying. Maybe he needed to apologize to himself, for losing sight of his path, for opening the door for his own demons to come in.

"If you can hear me, please help me," Silas whispered.

Silence drowned out his last words. He felt something, a presence hovering over him like an umbrella. The room instantly felt cold. Freaking out, he jumped from the bed.

His phone rang. Ejiro. The answer to his prayer?

"You have good news?" Silas asked, breathless.

"Afraid not. They are pulling your movies and drama series, claiming that you're a liability to the Agency."

Silas nearly threw his phone at the wall. "They can't do that."

"The big-boy lawyers from the network came by the office. Your endorsements, commercials are on pause, people calling for a boycott. They're losing money, so they want you out—"

"This is bull. I didn't do anything." If Nollywood barred him from acting, was that it for him? Did God want him to leave acting behind?

"It gets worse," Ejiro said. "They plan to sue for breach of contract."

"Then I'll sue them too."

"Calm down. I scheduled a meeting with Mr. Johnson—"

"For what? He and his trifling wife are the reason I'm in this mess." Silas paced the carpet in front of his bed. He couldn't keep playing defense with these people.

"Just give me this week. I'll talk to him, tell him you're on your way back."

Silas kicked the suitcase beside the bed, wishing it was Johnson's ugly face. "I don't care what you tell him. You and them lawyers need to do your jobs. Johnson and his nonsense wife know I didn't do anything."

"I'm doing the best I can," Ejiro mumbled.

Silas stopped pacing. Why was he yelling at an innocent person? If Ejiro turned on him, all hope was lost. He needed his team to keep fighting hard for him.

"I'm—" The line made a sound like it was trying to reconnect the call. Silas checked his phone, waiting for the call to resume, but it didn't. He hung up and called Ejiro back. The line kept ringing. He called again and again.

After the fifth time, Silas went to get more coffee. Ejiro was probably pissed at the way he talked to him. After all, right now was the best time for Ejiro to drop Silas before Ejiro got pulled deeper into his legal woes.

"Really God?" he mumbled. "I finally ask you for something and this is how you respond?"

Silas slammed down his mug and opened the fridge. Time for another bottle of vodka.

6

Ibelema couldn't look away from the man. No one made a sound as he acted out the lines she'd penned. With the wounded expression in his eyes, he really was the broken Reverend in the flesh, grieving over the son who had strayed and now stood against him.

She knew every line of the script, but couldn't help the thrill that passed through her at every pause and quiver of Tonye's rich bass voice as he fought to hold his rising anger. During the scene with the Rev and his wife in the hotel room, Tonye adlibbed and pounded his chest. "After we took him as our own and gave him everything..." He bowed his head as if praying. Then, the deep rumbling of a man wailing rose to feverish laughter. Tonye looked up, his face like stone, and yet somehow his eyes were soft with tears.

"I will bury him," he growled.

"Jesus," came a voice behind her. Applause thundered against the walls of the gym.

Tonye looked around and joined his palms together before settling his gaze on her. Ibelema clapped because he deserved it, and the corner of his mouth twitched, looking pleased with her reaction. He walked over with a triumphant smile.

"I definitely can't pay you," IB deadpanned, and the room exploded in laughter.

"She says that to everyone," Daniel said, shaking Tonye's hand.

"It was a really good performance," Ibelema went on.

Tonye watched her like a man used to praise. She hadn't expected him to show up, and he was one of the first to arrive, eyes red as if he'd spent all night rehearsing.

"The script is amazing," Tonye cut in, staring at her like he had more to say.

Ibelema searched the room for Efe. She needed her wing-woman to block this guy before he started talking nonsense. At least he wasn't checking her out like those creepy Nigerian guys who came to church just to get a date. Tonye's eyes right now were those of a man who wanted something different from her. He was totally changed from the guy at the restaurant.

"I owe you something," he said.

Whatever it is you can keep it, she wanted to say. How could he look like a boy with that deep voice? "Just glad you're here to help out," she said, with a brief nod.

"Glad to be of help to you."

Efe bounced over to Ibelema with a wide smile. "Cute," Efe whispered too loudly, before shaking Tonye's hand and introducing herself.

Ibelema studied Tonye while he was distracted. Efe's

standards were pretty high, so if she said a guy was cute, then he was a real looker. Ibelema had to admit the man oozed so much effortless charm, she felt guilty just looking at him. Still, he wasn't exactly her type. Regular height with smooth brown skin, not dark chocolate like Kenneth.

Last night, she found a dating book Kenneth had given her the week before they were set to start marriage counseling at the church. She'd stared at the book for a while, thinking how in the world their relationship had fallen apart so fast. Then she went to the garage and dumped the book in the big trash can.

"Any friend of IB is cool with me." Tonye flashed his pearly whites at her. He had great teeth. More people approached him to rave about his performance. He seemed friendly enough. Maybe Ibelema had misjudged him all these years. She walked to her laptop on the desk by the soundboard.

Daniel nudged her arm. "Congrats. You found the Rev."

"I honestly can't believe it," Ibelema replied.

"Should I brief him on his first scene?" Daniel asked.

"You think we can start shooting today?"

"He seems ready. I'll go ask him."

Ibelema let out a deep breath of relief. Now that their cast was complete, the finish line was within reach. Taking a seat by the desk, she pulled up the filming schedule on her laptop. They would need to hustle to make the deadline.

Efe stopped by the desk with a puzzled expression. "Tonye looks sort of familiar." She tilted her head as if thinking. "I can't figure out where I've seen him."

"Maybe in a Nigerian film," Ibelema said. Was Tonye more famous than she thought?

"It's not that. He just seems like someone I know." Efe's face broke into a wide grin. "He's amazing. How did you convince the perfect guy to do this without getting paid?"

Ibelema faked a bright smile. "With my winning personality," she teased, and Efe's deadpan made her chuckle. It didn't matter why Tonye joined them. The way he kept looking at her, he probably had a sketchy reason anyway.

"Just go easy on him," Efe continued. "We don't want him to quit, Madame Director."

"He won't."

"Why are you so sure?"

Tonye looked her way, eyes dancing as if someone told him a joke. Ibelema smiled back at him as he walked toward her. He did have a cute smile.

"Your name is Ibelema?" he asked her, clearly excited.

"Yeah. Why?"

"My Sugar," he said. "Kay never told me your dad is from Bonny."

She frowned. "Sugar" was a loose interpretation of her name. The real meaning was more intimate—my love. "Wait, you're from Bonny?"

Tonye nodded with boyish enthusiasm. "I'm glad to help out a relative."

"Right..." This was usually the point guys like him asked her out on a date.

"But I'm not just helping you for you."

"Oh, why are you helping then?" Ibelema pinned her gaze on her laptop to escape his penetrating eyes. Efe, in her rotten timing, had already walked away to talk with the others.

"I want something," he replied.

She hesitated to ask. "What do you want, Tonye?"

"You." His mouth spread in an effortless, melt-your-heart sort of smile. "I want you, Ibe-le-ma."

Her jaw dropped so wide, she had to remind herself to close her mouth. She never expected Tonye to take the most direct approach, and the way he sounded out every syllable of her name so intimately sent a tingle down her spine.

"Let me take you out on a date," he carried on.

Ibelema steeled herself, her face becoming neutral again. "I don't know you."

"Easily remedied. Kay and Barbara were trying to hook us up anyway."

"I never agreed to that." This guy really was bad through and through.

"Well, you told me you'd make this worth my while. Are you going back on what you said?"

Why on earth did she tell him that? "No, but I don't like being played. You already said you would help, but now you're saying you won't."

"I didn't say I wouldn't help—I'm playing the Rev either way. I'm just asking you to think about going out with me."

Ibelema stared at Tonye. He was helping her, so she couldn't just shut him down. And it wasn't as if she hadn't expected him to come onto her in some way, especially after what Barbara said at the restaurant. What was the harm of going on just one date?

"I'll think about it," she said finally.

He clapped before rubbing his hands together. "So, when do we start filming?"

Ibelema tried not to look excited. "Today, if you're ready."

"I'm always ready." Daniel approached and the men bumped fists.

"I already told him about the prayer scene in the park," Daniel said. "We can go check it now. I'll ride with Tonye and fill him in."

"I was meaning to talk to you anyway," Tonye said.

"About what?" Ibelema asked, not liking this buddy vibe between them. Something told her Tonye wanted to talk about her.

"None of your business." Daniel winked and slapped Tonye's back before the two of them walked away from her. "We'll see you there, Boss."

As Ibelema watched them leave, Tonye looked back at her with that mischievous smile, a silent threat of trouble to come. She needed to talk to her friend. Why would Barbara think she and Tonye could be a good fit? She made a mental note to Google him and find out everything she could about the man.

7

"Cut," IB's voice broke the tense silence of their fourth take of the scene.

Silas clenched his jaw, slightly irritated. Before she'd stopped the action this time, he knew the correction was coming. This power trip felt like hazing to see if he could take her criticism. She was obviously trying to show him who was the boss—otherwise, there was no way he could keep getting so much of the scene wrong.

The first day of shooting, IB had pulled him aside to adjust the way he'd called Pastor Samuel's last name. The day after that, she pointed out how he walked too "young and loose" for a middle-aged man, whatever that meant. Earlier today, she wanted him to tone down his reactions a little. And now, she had stopped again. What did she want to say now, that he was breathing wrong?

When she squinted at him, Silas couldn't stop himself from

flinching. No woman had ever made him feel like this much of a screw-up. He started filming a week ago and realized now that more than anything he wanted to hear IB compliment him. She was always praising Efe, Daniel, and pretty much everyone else while she never gave him a kind word. Maybe he shouldn't have asked her on a date so early in the game. She still hadn't even given him a real response. Was she buying time until he shot all his scenes and she didn't need him anymore?

"Something's off," IB said, with a distracted look.

Silas felt like he was coming down with something. He had arrived at the church building hours ago to shoot the first confrontation between Samuel and the Rev. Everyone was staring, including Obadiah--the guy playing Samuel—who kept tripping over his lines, but IB hardly corrected the amateur or the others.

"What's off?" He tried not to sound irritated.

IB tapped her lips. "Do you understand what an antagonist means?"

She was taking this too far. "You do know I'm—"

"You're not being ruthless enough," Daniel jumped in. "You're reacting to a betrayal by someone you still consider a son to you. You said you'll bury him, remember?"

"Exactly," IB agreed, with a firm nod. "Tonye, I know you're used to playing heroes, but you're the villain here. You should be angry that Samuel is backstabbing you. The way you're talking to him is too friendly."

Silas bit back a retort. "I thought that was what I was doing." He'd never played the lead villain before. "You told me to tone it down, remember?"

"I still want the raw emotion," she said, smiling patiently as if dealing with a child. "I know it's challenging for you to play a villain, but we've all been bad guys in someone else's story before. I'm sure someone has royally pissed you off until you wanted to pay them back big time. That's the energy we need for this scene."

Silas adjusted his glasses. He didn't need any more of her pep talks.

"Let's take a break," she said.

"A break would be nice," Efe said, followed by murmurs from the others probably tired of shooting in the cramped office space.

Silas blew a hard breath through his lips. It was his fault the scene was dragging. He didn't want to take a break, and from the look on IB's face, she wanted to keep going, but everyone was leaving the room.

IB sighed as she walked out of the office. Silas followed Daniel to the vending machine and got a coke.

"Why do you seem nervous?" Daniel asked.

"I'm not," Silas said through clenched teeth. He was the only trained actor, so what would he have to be nervous about? Everyone else on set was a friend of IB's she recruited to be part of the project. Since she had gotten this many people to volunteer their time, it was either that they really liked her, or she'd offered to share the prize money with them in case the film won any awards.

"Do you feel the Rev is a bad person?" Daniel pressed him suddenly.

"No, how could he be?" Silas replied. "The man is a true Christian. He truly loves God."

"And yet, there's something absurd about the way he's going about things."

"True." Pastor Samuel wasn't wrong in wanting the church to be more straightforward about financial matters and not prioritize the number of converts or members over the actual spiritual growth of the people already in the church. If the Rev truly loved God, how could he be against Samuel's way of thinking? Why was he tied to the old method of doing things when he knew in his heart it wasn't the right way? The Rev had prayed for revival for so long, yet now that the answer was in front of him, he wanted nothing to do with it.

"Even good people do bad things when they're desperate," Daniel said, turning to look Silas square in the face. "Do you ever feel desperate, angry?"

Angry? Anger didn't begin to explain what Silas felt toward Maxwell and Jeanie Johnson for ruining his career, or the Nigerian public for throwing him away like he was nothing.

Daniel laughed. "A quiet boiling rage on the verge of exploding, but never fully giving in to the madness."

"Exactly." IB walked into the building through the back door that led into the parking lot, glancing between the two men. "I'm not sure what you guys are talking about, but your face right now is exactly how you need to play the Rev." She snapped her fingers, clearly excited. "Let's take off for today and regroup on Saturday."

Before Silas could say anything, IB raised a hand to silence him. "I believe in you. Just take a day off and you'll see." Without another word, she hurried to the office room where the shooting was taking place.

Silas shook his head. "Is she like this all the time?"

Daniel grinned like he knew what Tonye was thinking. "You sure you're ready for a woman like her?"

Silas had to smile at that. When he first saw IB with Daniel, he thought something may have been going on between them. The two struck him as friends who had tried to date but it didn't work out, yet they somehow remained cool.

"I was sort of into IB at first," Daniel revealed. "But I quickly got the vibe that she didn't feel the same way. But it's cool, we wouldn't have been able to work together if we had that between us. So now we're homies."

Silas nodded silently, still wondering to himself why she didn't give Daniel a chance. Daniel seemed like IB's type—laidback and easy to talk to—while IB was the girl who sat in front of class because she thought everyone else was a distraction, and plowed her way through life without giving much thought to those she offended. She had this *gragra*-intense nature that made everything dramatic, but she didn't like any sort of drama in her life.

That first day he showed up on set and rode with Daniel to the park, Daniel had given Silas a run-down of the project. Everyone on the team had volunteered so IB worked around their schedules and paid out of her pocket for their meals during long shoots. This film wasn't just some pet project, but the beginning of her screenwriting and directing career. A Week on the Mountain was her baby. No wonder she'd glared at him when he'd unintentionally made fun of her film at the suya spot, or the way her eyes lit up with pride when he nailed the audition for the Reverend.

"You're a good man," Silas said. "I don't see how I could be just friends with a woman like that."

Daniel smiled. "I'm going to choose to believe you mean that in the best way possible."

Silas bit back the joke at the tip of his tongue. Daniel seemed like a guy who took women seriously, so he didn't want him to get the wrong idea.

Daniel bumped Silas' shoulder with his fist. "That's why you have to nail this part," he reminded Silas as they walked to the back door leading to the parking lot. "And for the record, you seem like a good guy too."

"No, I'm not."

"Why? Because of the scandal?"

Silas whirled around to face him in surprise. He knew?

"I watched your last movie with my aunt," Daniel said. "She's looking forward to Red Avenue."

A bewildered Silas swallowed hard. "Cool," he said, not knowing what else to say. If Daniel knew, IB would too, along with everyone else, and they'd probably judge him with their churchy ways. Still, it didn't feel like Daniel was tripping about it. Had Daniel known he was Silas, not Tonye, from the start?

"There's no way you did something like that," Daniel continued in a calm voice. "And even if you did, the you that's standing before me right now isn't the same person."

Silas laughed nervously in an attempt to quell his nerves. "You just met me."

"Sure, but the Tonye I'm seeing now and the Silas from before can't be the same person."

Silas couldn't wrap his head around Daniel's meaning. It wasn't the first time in the week he'd known him that he thought the guy was weird. And yet there was something refreshing about his straightforward way of saying things. That same day, on their ride to the park, Silas had asked Daniel if IB would let him invest in the film, and Daniel told him not to worry about her approval because they needed money for the edits.

"If you help us make this film a success, I'll help you too," Daniel spoke, interrupting Silas' thoughts again. He glanced at Silas as if he was waiting for him to say something more.

Silas knew what Daniel wanted him to say, but another question burned inside of him, and knowing the truth would mean he had to do something about it.

"How could you know what I was like before?" Silas blurted out, and Daniel just smiled.

When Silas talked to Kay later that night, he made sure to ask about Daniel and IB.

"They're just good friends," Kay said. "Daniel is even closer to Kimani than IB. He used to be a very different type of dude before he got saved."

Kay said they would talk some more when Silas came over. Barbara's persistence finally won out and he'd accepted an invitation for dinner at their house. Two weeks had passed since he encountered the stranger at his hotel, and Silas wanted to believe the man had given up by now.

The next day, Silas drove to Kay's place. He parked in the turnaround courtyard and scanned the street to make sure he wasn't followed.

Kay's house was a massive two-story surrounded by well-tended grounds and majestic palm trees swaying in the light breeze. A winding pebbled path led to the front door, where Kay was waiting with a bear hug.

Barbara appeared behind Kay in the doorway, beckoning them inside with a finger on her lips because Princess Tiwa was sleeping.

As Silas entered the house, a flowery scent tickled his nose. It smelled like home. Their house was an open floor with a humongous kitchen, a dazzling granite island, and a fridge that reflected pictures of Tiwa through her first fifteen months. She was adorable, a perfect blend of her parents.

In the dining room, Barbara set the table with banga soup and plantain fufu, and Silas gratefully demolished his meal. It was the most he had eaten in years. Once they were done, Kay took Silas to the study and asked him for a favor.

"You want me to watch Tiwa with IB?" Silas repeated slowly, trying to process what Kay had just told him.

"There's this all-day marriage conference on Saturday in the Woodlands, and Barb wanted to go, so I got us in." Barbara's mom was busy with a convention, so IB agreed to help in her stead. "It's really me doing you a favor, so don't mess this up. We'll be back by 7, latest 8."

Silas couldn't help the smiling at the thought of spending uninterrupted time alone with IB. Well, not exactly alone—but Tiwa had to sleep at some point, right?

"My mother-in-law normally watches Tiwa, but with the convention—don't ask—seems like she always has something going on." Distracted, Kay checked his desktop. "Barbara deserves this. It was really hard for her postpartum, breastfeeding and other stuff. I mean, the constant grind of raising a kid just gets to you. And when grandparents aren't flexible, it gets even tougher."

Kay looked sad as his words trailed off. Silas thought to put a hand on his shoulder. A lot must have happened to his friend without him knowing it while he was busy chasing an acting career that now amounted to nothing.

Ashamed, Silas caught a picture on Kay's desk of Kay, Barbara, and baby Tiwa when she looked just days or weeks old. The uninhibited joy in his friend's eyes made him look away. At thirty-two, what did he have? No wife, no kids...what would he do from now on?

"Please take your wife to the conference," Silas said. "Whatever you guys need from me, I'm here to help." He owed Kay for forgiving him for not being at his wedding, and believing in him back then and now.

Both of the men's heads turned when the door to the study opened, and Barbara walked in hand-in-hand with Tiwa. His goddaughter gave Silas a suspicious look as she waddled across the carpet into Daddy's arms, making Kay the happiest he ever saw him.

"So, Tonye, what are your plans for my best friend?" Barbara eyed him as if she expected him to say the wrong thing. "How do you feel about IB?"

The question felt like a fist rammed his throat. Whichever way he sliced or diced it, IB made so much sense. But she was Barbara's best friend. He couldn't just woo her, and then let her down easy if she turned out not to be what he expected. And that was the problem. Never knowing who a person really was until you were already drowning in their waves.

"IB is the most incredible woman I've ever met." The words jumped out of him, but it was the truth. "I go to sleep thinking about her. I wake up thinking about her."

Watching Barbara's smile, he knew he'd said what she wanted to hear, but she was still looking at him like he hadn't answered the question.

"I'm not sure how to explain what I feel, but I..." He knew what he wanted to say, but didn't know how to say it. "I would hate myself if years from now I ran into her with someone else. Every time I look at her, I wonder how it would feel to be the man she loves."

Barbara's face split in a grin. "I knew I always liked you." She exchanged looks with Kay, who blinked at her in shock. "Did you think your boy could talk like this?"

Kay shook his head. "IB has slain the man." He pumped his fist, and Tiwa screamed for joy.

"Slain in the Spirit," Barbara joked.

"It's on," Kay whooped. "Wherever or whenever y'all get married, we're there."

Marriage? "Take it easy, bro."

Silas laughed. For the first time in his life, the thought of getting married didn't sound so bad after all.

8

Ibelema's eyes flitted between the camera in her hands to her cousin Michael. "Am I allowed to keep this? Isn't it worth thousands of dollars?" Ibelema wondered, touching the nondescript package label. Someone had sent the camera to her temporary workplace, and Michael brought it to her.

Efe chuckled as she stacked the flyers for the upcoming youth conference. She had dropped by the youth center with Jackie and Chanel. Jackie was playing the role of a famous gospel worship leader who joined forces with Pastor Samuel in Ibelema's film.

"You keep looking at the camera as if it'll magically tell you who sent it," Jackie said.

"Whoa," Michael said, holding up his phone to reveal a Google search. "This thing is like five thousand bucks. Filmmakers really love it." He placed the camera back in its case like it was a golden egg.

"That's wild," Efe whistled.

"Who do you think is behind it?" Chanel asked, in her cute voice.

Ibelema roughed Chanel's silky hair and Chanel gave a shy smile. It was nice to see her hanging out. Jackie and Efe were taking Chanel to dinner, and it looked like working on the film together had brought the three of them closer.

"The real question is how did it end up at my mom's office," Michael wondered.

"A secret admirer," Jackie said with swoon. She was a sucker for anything romance, and the steamier the better. After reading IB's script, Jackie complained that there weren't any love scenes and suggested edits that had no place in their Christian drama thriller.

"It's obviously someone who loves movies and thought to support our project," Ibelema responded. "Whoever they are, God bless them."

Jackie coughed. "I think the guy's hoping you'd bless him." She giggled with Efe and Michael. "Praise Jesus."

"IB's so cute," Efe said. "This whole time we've been working on your film using Michael's phone, no one stepped up to buy you a camera. Who else could it be if not a secret admirer?"

"Sounds like Efe knows who it is," Michael teased.

Ibelema tried to read Efe's bright eyes. They were probably thinking the same thing. Tonye. Still, to buy such an expensive gift, did he have money to burn like that? She hadn't even gotten back to him about the date yet. She figured they should focus on finishing the movie, then she would be in a better frame of mind to possibly go on a date with him. Talking to Barbara about Tonye had made her relax more around him. Barbara's advice? Go on the date, and if Ibelema wasn't feeling it, she could let him down easy.

"It's definitely someone who likes you," Efe said.

Ibelema rolled her eyes. "Hate to disappoint y'all, but this isn't some cheesy romance."

"What's wrong with romance?" Jackie asked. "Romance makes the world go round."

Michael tapped the camera. "I always knew you would marry a rich guy. Look out for me when he comes through."

Ibelema rubbed her forehead, wondering about the mystery gift. The package wasn't labeled. Aunty Osagie said she didn't see who dropped it off, but if they checked the CCTV recording, wouldn't the person show up?

"I think it's Tonye," Chanel stated like it was a fact.

Everyone looked at Ibelema. "It's not him," she said. "Why would he?"

"You think we're all blind?" Jackie rolled her eyes. "Everyone sees how that man looks at you." Efe and Michael nodded in agreement.

"I'm the director," Ibelema said. "He has to look at me." Even Chanel laughed at that one.

"I think he's awesome," Jackie said, with a cattish grin. "We all make mistakes, but with him, you just nitpick the man differently."

"Because I expect more from him." Ibelema thought it best not to tell the crew that Tonye was a Nollywood actor. Knowing his real identity would make the girls only fawn over him more.

"Tonye's a pro," Michael said. "He knows how to capture the camera, and he always has the right voice level to catch the mic. And his audition was the best ever."

Ibelema moved the stack of flyers to the side of the desk. "Is standing and talking in front of a camera rocket science?" she muttered to no one in particular, pouting when all four of them nodded with smiles.

During his first shoot, Tonye seemed pissed when she corrected him about his tone. But after that, he performed better with each scene. He was already a great Rev, but Ibelema kept pushing him because she knew he could pull off a near-perfect portrayal of what she imagined in her head.

"I'm tough on him because he's good," Ibelema corrected.

"Then give him a break," Efe said. "His role isn't easy and he's not doing it for money."

"Last I checked we ain't getting paid," Jackie blurted.

"But she tells us how much she appreciates us," Chanel countered.

"Do you say that to Tonye?" Efe turned to Ibelema. "That you're only hard on him because he's talented?"

Ibelema frowned. "He'll just get a bigger head."

"Right," Efe said. "You can't tell him that he's doing a good job because your overly-spiritual self won't let you be nice to any guy you're feeling."

Ibelema nearly choked on her response. "Feeling who?"

Jackie pointed at her in glee. "I knew it—he's totally your type."

"As if." Ibelema shot to her feet. "What are we even talking about?"

"I don't see it," Michael said. "Daniel's more your speed."

Ibelema glared at him. "Daniel is like my brother."

"Spiritual brother," Efe corrected.

"What does that even mean?" Jackie asked.

"It means she friend-zoned him, but worse—she bro-zoned him," Michael replied. "I hate it when y'all do that."

"And I really hate when guys say that," Efe retorted.

Jackie threw up her hands. "This sister-brother talk is destroying us, people. How will we ever find love if we keep friend-zoning our fellow believers?"

Michael slung his arm around Jackie. "Exactly, so, Jackie—"

"Boy, please." Jackie punched Michael's arm and he stumbled away from her in mock-injury.

"Daniel likes Eden," Chanel announced.

Ibelema burst out laughing. Chanel's powers of observation were scary. Kimani was the first to notice how Daniel always acted strangely around Eden, but when they asked Daniel about it, he said they were "wilding." Like they didn't know how he usually behaved detached around women.

"Eden?" Jackie asked as if trying to remember the name.

"The white girl?" Michael added.

"Yeah," Ibelema said. "She doesn't go to our church."

"How do you know Eden?" Efe asked.

"House of Hope," Chanel replied.

"One of y'all need to hook a brother up." Michael sighed, and Jackie doubled over in laughter.

"You need serious prayers first," Ibelema said, glancing at her wristwatch for the time. Barbara had asked for help touching up her braids and insisted on coming over to Ibelema's house while Kay hung out with Tiwa.

The others didn't look like they would be done soon, so Ibelema left them at the youth center. By the time she got home, Barbara was already there with Mom and Aunty Osagie at the dining table inspecting *ankara*, velvet, and lace.

Ibelema took Barbara upstairs to her room and they got started on Barbara's hair. At first, they talked about church, then the conversation somehow landed on Tonye again.

"They've known each other since KC," Barbara explained of the actor's connection to Kay. "Went to law school together."

"Tonye's a lawyer?" Ibelema's fingers stalled at the end of the long braid. "How in the world did a lawyer end up in Nollywood?"

"What's wrong with Nollywood?"

"Cheesy characters, poor video quality, crappy plotlines," Ibelema rattled off the list of issues on her free hand. "Nigerians are some of the most talented people in the world, and yet we can do so much better."

"You're so bougie. Some Naija movies are quite good, like Finding Mr. Forever."

Ibelema mimed like she might vomit. Barbara only loved that movie because Tonye had a small role in it. The same tired plotline had Korean, Spanish, Chinese, and Filipino adaptations. "With the Ebola pandemic, religious extremists, corruption at every level, or our rich history, why are we as a nation not making movies about those things, instead of a crazy witch who doesn't want to see her son marry because she doesn't want to be alone?"

"Not every time activism, IB." Barbara sighed. "Sometimes we just want a simple rom-com."

"Now you sound like Jackie."

"And you sound like a movie snob," she shot back. "Why are you so against adding a romantic scene to your film? Does it scratch your throat to see people in love? Can't Samuel and his wife show some PDA, Ms. Romance Scrooge?"

"You guys want more than just kissing." Ibelema nudged Barbara's head forward. "Plus, Efe thanked me there's no kissing."

"That one, would it be such a bad thing for her to kiss Obadiah?"

"If you have the opportunity to reach your audience with a compelling message, why waste it on a distraction like kissing?"

Barbara frowned. "Is that why you haven't gone on a date yet with Tonye?"

Ibelema froze with the braid in her hand. "How did we go from—"

"Real talk, IB, what do you think about him?" Ibelema tugged on a braid in reply, and Barbara jerked. "Aren't you curious about him?"

"I already told you I would go on a date with him."

"Then you shouldn't have a problem with him coming by this Saturday."

Her heart jumped. "What do you mean Saturday?"

"He's coming to help you watch Tiwa, so you two will have plenty of time to bond."

"Barb, how could you? You know, I could just decide not to come, you know?"

Barbara pouted. "You wouldn't do that to Tiwa."

Ibelema smacked Barbara's head and stood up from the chair. "You're so annoying."

"Where are you going?"

"I'm done. Look in the mirror."

Barbara held up the hand mirror to check the back of her hair before wrapping Ibelema in a tight hug. "They're perfect, IB—just like you."

"Girl, go to your house." Ibelema shrugged her off. "Setting me up like that. You're lucky it's for my baby."

"You'll thank me later."

"When? After he breaks my heart?"

Barbara placed a hand to her chest, mock swooning. "See? You really do like him."

"In your dreams."

Barbara grabbed her bag. "Don't worry. Tonye won't do that

to you," she assured Ibelema.

"How do you know?"

"He's whipped already. I saw it in his face when he talked about you," she called as she rushed out of the room.

Ibelema chased Barbara down the stairs and outside to the driveway, tapping on the window as Barbara slipped into her car. "Stop acting like a brat. Just tell me what he said."

Barbara started the engine and rolled down the window. "Only that you're the most incredible woman he's ever met."

Ibelema blinked back her surprise. "Stop messing with me."

"It's going to be great, IB," Barbara said in a sing-song voice, looking over her shoulder to reverse down the driveway. "Just let go and let God," she quoted one of Kimani's favorite lines.

Ibelema watched the car peel down the street and turn the corner, still stunned in silence. Tonye would never say that, not after all the trouble she'd given him. When she entered the house, Mom and Aunty Osagie watched her with curious eyes from the dining table.

Aunty held up a navy blue and pink *ankara*. "This is the *asoebi* for Bella's wedding in two weeks."

Ibelema had lost count of the weddings and parties she'd been forced to attend because her parents had claimed acquaintances from every part of Nigeria as family friends. Bella wasn't her friend, so why did she have to show face there? Thank God she had Phoebe's wedding as the perfect excuse.

"I can't go," Ibelema said. "The Teka wedding is that same day." Her parents planned to attend the ceremony before hurrying off to Bella's wedding, which would most likely start at least an hour late, given that Nigerians only kept to Nigerian time.

Mom raised her hands in supplication. "Thank God for this Teka wedding."

When Papa and Mama Teka died, it was a rough time for the entire church, as the Tekas were heavily involved in several ministries. When Phoebe got engaged to Abe, the church was buzzing for the wedding. After all the division the church had experienced in the past year, the Teka wedding couldn't have come at a better time.

"But you should still try to stop by Bella's wedding," Mom went on. "Osagie said there'll be some nice Nigerian boys there. Or have you forgotten the dream I–"

"Sister," Aunty jumped in, giving her a look. "Let the young woman do her thing. These people, do they come when we're doing our own celebrations?"

"They will come to Ibelema's wedding now," Mom said in determination.

"Does she even want them to come?" Aunty asked.

Ibelema tiptoed away from them before her mom turned on her again. She went upstairs and shut the door to her room. One day, she would be free from all their obligations and questions. As much as she loved her parents, they needed to understand she had her own life and her own friends.

Ibelema clenched and unclenched her fist, her fingers aching from braiding Barbara's hair. As she lay down on her bed, she couldn't help smiling. Did Tonye really say that about her?

She picked up her phone and scrolled to his saved number. The guy thought he was slick. He gave her his number just in case she needed to reach him for "any updates on the shooting schedule."

"Saturday," she whispered, with a smile. "I guess you'll get your date after all, Tonye Banigo."

9

On Saturday, Silas arrived at Kay's house just as his friend was ushering Barbara into the Benz. IB's blue Beetle was parked on the turnaround, and she stood on the winding path carrying Tiwa. Silas waved at her, trying not to appear excited that he was spending the whole day with her.

Once the parents left, Tiwa started crying. IB held her, and Silas tried to be helpful, but he couldn't understand how such a tiny person could make that much noise.

"She's hungry," IB said, gently bouncing Tiwa in her arms. "She was too sleepy to eat the first time. Could you please get her bottle from the fridge while I change her diaper?" IB shuffled past him toward the stairs before pausing to look back. "You know how to warm a bottle, right?"

Silas winced as Tiwa's crying got louder. "It can't be that hard."

If doubt could be personified, it would be IB giving him a long look. Only God could help him now. Why was she sexy without trying?

"Just wait until I change her diaper," she said, hurrying up the stairs. Clearly, she thought him incompetent.

Silas opened the fridge and fished out a pre-made milk bottle. Were these things microwavable? Who had the genius thought to make baby bottles out of plastic? He checked the white cabinets and found a mug to pour the milk into.

IB returned downstairs with a monitor in her hand. "She's asleep," she announced, and put the bottle back in the fridge. "Thank God."

Silas smiled at the sleeping baby on the monitor. "Well done," he said, watching her walk into the living room. From the back or the front, the woman was a sight to behold. She had a funny way of walking, as if most of her weight was shifted to the front part of her feet. Her curvy hips swayed like she was about to break into dance. His mind wandered to having her softness against him, what it would feel like to kiss her.

She glanced over her shoulder and he looked away. Guilty as charged. She'd totally caught him checking her out.

Silas trailed her to the living room, where Tiwa's toys were scattered everywhere. "What do we now?" he asked.

"We wait for her to wake up." IB walked past him to the curated bookshelf near the window. "Her first nap usually lasts an hour. Then we start the whole process all over again."

Meaning they had an uninterrupted hour together. Silas sat on the black leather sectional, racking his brain for what to say next. Even though he usually avoided parties, he could small-talk anyone if he had to, but at the moment he couldn't think of anything that wouldn't sound embarrassing.

Defeated, Silas faced the TV. Better to keep quiet than make a fool of himself so early in their day. What was up with this awkwardness? Why was he so self-conscious, fearing that if he took the wrong step, IB might not want anything to do with him? The thought of her disliking him made his stomach sink.

"So...did you have anything you wanted to do?" IB asked, interrupting his thoughts.

Silas jerked back to attention, sitting up straight. He could think of several things he wanted to do to her. No, what the heck was he thinking right now? He managed to shake his head.

"Do you want to play Ludo, or Snakes and Ladders while we wait?"

He raised his brows at the mention of the famous game. "What do you know about Ludo?"

IB grabbed a stack of board games nearby. "You're about to find out."

"Challenge accepted." Silas was the notorious Ludo champion in his secondary school. He sat on the rug, and she joined him at the coffee table shoved against the sofa to leave room for Tiwa's boxes of toys. They picked colors and IB stationed her pieces on each home base.

"I can already guess your plan to cheat," he said.

She brushed his hand away from the dice, a jolt running up his arm at the unexpected physical touch. "Ladies first." IB dragged her piece across the board. Even her little fingers were cute. "Your turn," she said. Her pretty brown eyes sparkled like she was having fun.

"When was the last time you were in Nigeria?"

She appeared to think about it. "Not since college. Why did you come to Houston after all this time?"

Silas looked up to see her smiling at him. She was curious

about him—good. "It's complicated."

"I know that much." She rolled the dice. "You're kind of a mystery."

He stared hard into her coffee-brown eyes and she didn't look away. "I could say the same about you, Ibelema Pepple."

Her brows went up. "I'm an open book."

"Really?"

"Go on, ask me anything."

"You're good, I'll pass." Was this a trick?

"Come on, we're here all day so you might as well. What do you want to know?"

He leaned back against the couch. "Fine, I'll bite. Why are you still single?"

IB smacked a hand over her mouth, muffling a scream. "No, you didn't."

"It's a fair question."

"No, it's not. You don't play fair."

"You told me to ask anything."

She rolled her eyes. "Fine. I'm single because the last guy I dated used me as a test."

"A test?" Silas asked in confusion. "A test for what?"

"Not sure. I'll let you know when I dissect it by writing a story about it." Her mouth pushed in like she was holding back laughter. She was messing with him. "But yeah, I guess you could say the test was successful. He's engaged now, and I've decided I've had enough of men."

Silas fought to keep his face straight. "He was a tool."

"Unfortunately, I've always attracted those kinds of guys, because the other ones—" she made air quotes with her fingers. "The good ones apparently find me intimidating and unapproachable."

Silas watched her long, slender fingers trail the board. "You're not unapproachable."

"You didn't say I wasn't intimidating."

"I mean, that's not a word I'd use to describe you."

"What words would you use then?" she asked, in the sweetest voice.

"Let me see." He tapped his chin, pretending to think. "Amazing, breathtaking...sexy."

Her eyes blew up at him. Right on cue, the baby monitor turned on, the sound of Tiwa's wailing cutting through the silence.

IB bounded up the stairs. "You're losing, so you get to change her diaper."

Minutes later, Silas wished he'd tried harder to win the game. Wrangling Tiwa for a diaper change was ridiculous. He really didn't want to hold her in place, but she kept wiggling on the changing mat. IB was cackling when he finally got the new diaper underneath Tiwa, but the toddler skillfully turned on her stomach and rolled away from him. Then Tiwa got up and ran toward the front door. Silas watched in wonder as IB chased her down and brought her back.

IB nudged him aside. Within seconds, Tiwa had on a new diaper and was babbling away.

Silas followed them to the kitchen. "How do parents manage in America? Don't they have live-in nannies over here?" House-helps had mostly raised him as a kid since his dad was always working.

"Barb's way too paranoid for that. And honestly, with all the stories I've heard about nannies, I wouldn't have one either. There's nothing like bonding with your child over dirty diapers and sleepless nights." IB opened the fridge with Tiwa perched on her hip.

Silas grabbed the fridge handle. "I can do it."

Both IB and Tiwa looked at him, as if to say: Stay in your lane. He grabbed the baby bottle with confidence. "I got this. Just go play with her in the living room. It'll be ready in a minute."

"It'll take longer than that," IB said, pointing to a strange appliance on the kitchen counter. "Just stick it in the bottle warmer." As she went to the living room, she was walking weirdly, as if her legs were tied together.

Silas put the bottle in the warmer and pressed the red button. "Are you okay?"

"I need to pee." She was so cute.

"Go, I'll watch her."

IB put Tiwa by the couch and shuffled down the hallway. Tiwa began to follow her godmother until she got distracted by her teddy bear lying on the floor. She picked up the worn-out stuffed bear and swung it around wildly.

Silas stayed close to her, but Tiwa paid him no attention to him. He had a lot of catching up to do. How could he miss the entire first year of her life? Maybe he could buy her a new bear.

The warmer beeped a noise and Silas went to get the bottle. He put it against his cheek and dripped some milk on his palm like he was taught to do in a movie once. The milk felt right, not too hot. IB wasn't back from the restroom yet. Tiwa was sitting by the couch with her back facing him. He could feed her and prove to IB that he could get some things right.

"Princess," he said, crouching to reach for her. "Time to eat—" Tiwa's eyes were glazed. The Ludo board was beside her. A yellow piece was missing. Tiwa made a wheezing sound.

Silas dropped the bottle and snatched her up. "Jesus, IB." He tilted Tiwa forward and pounded her back frantically.

"Ibelema!"

10

Ibelema stumbled out of the restroom to see Tonye holding Tiwa away from his body like she was a wild animal. His dark-blue polo was covered with a mysterious white liquid, and he was clearly shaken, while Tiwa looked pleased with herself.

"She almost swallowed one of the pieces," Tonye said. A yellow Ludo token sat in a puddle of Tiwa's vomit on the Persian rug. "I looked away for a moment—"

"It's not your fault," Ibelema assured him, though her heart was racing. She kissed Tiwa's cheek. "She's okay."

"I'm not," he mumbled. "Babies are ridiculous. Why would she eat that?"

Ibelema couldn't help chuckling at his serious expression. "You little troublemaker," Ibelema said, taking Tiwa from Tonye. Thank God she was alright. "This stays between us, okay?"

Tonye squatted by the mess. "How do you get vomit out of a

rug?"

"Soap and baking soda. But you need to change your shirt too."

His dark eyes grew wide behind his glasses. "First let's put this game back before we have another incident."

He wiped the dirty Ludo piece with his shirt, and he put the Ludo box on the bookcase, glancing at Tiwa every now and then as if still traumatized. Ibelema didn't have the heart to mention that Tiwa frequently put things in her mouth and would probably do so again before their evening together ended.

"That was my bad," she said, trying to make him relax. "Everything's usually childproofed."

He grabbed paper towels, and as he struggled to clean the vomit from his shirt, she caught a glimpse of the taut abs hiding underneath.

"Jesus," Ibelema breathed, flinching when she realized she'd spoken out loud, and Tonye looked at her with confusion. "Should I get one of Kay's shirts for you to wear while we wash yours?"

He smiled and she looked away, just in case he was crazy enough to take off his shirt right there in the living room. Why swoon over a six-pack like she hadn't seen one before? Efe and Jackie always gushed about ripped guys, and normally she found their thirst annoying, but now, she could understand the appeal. She had known Tonye was in shape, but seeing his body was something else.

"I have a tee in my car." He jogged out the front door, and returned minutes later wearing a vomit-free gray V-neck.

Tiwa wobbled to him with a big smile, hands outstretched, and Tonye picked her up with a grin of his own. Now that she'd marked him with her vomit, they were best of friends. Tiwa didn't let him put her down. He ended up feeding her the bottle, and she fell asleep in his arms.

Ibelema carried the sleeping toddler upstairs, and when she came down, she found him drinking a bottle of water. "Barb's going to be pissed," Ibelema whispered. "You're messing up her nap routine."

"You mean we?" Tonye chuckled. "She'll be a'ight. What else does she expect us to do?"

Ibelema shrugged. Who could argue with mothers and their unreasonable demands when it came to their kids? "Well, I'm sorry you got vomit on yourself."

"It's my fault if anything."

"How? I should have told you she likes to put stuff in her mouth."

Tonye watched her with soft eyes. "Are you one of those people who likes to take the blame for everything?"

Ibelema hesitated. Was that a thing? Most times, especially with her parents, she was the one to apologize first.

"That was random," she said, taking a seat on a stool by the counter. He sat next to her and did that licking-his-lips thing again. Ibelema dragged her eyes away.

"I'm sorry for being a jerk that first day we met," he said. "Hope you'll forgive me. I couldn't bear you being mad at me for anything."

Ibelema couldn't hide her smile. The moment was starting to feel like a scene from a cheesy rom-com. He was clearly trying to butter her up for the kill, and honestly, right now she didn't mind getting charmed by this man. They'd come a long way from the suya place.

"You're forgiven," she said.

He nudged her arm. "Thanks." His face brightened with that

easy smile and his gentle eyes seemed to sparkle.

Ibelema stood and held out her hand. "Let's have a do-over. I'm Ibelema Pepple and I'd like for you to be part of my film."

Tonye followed suit, taking her hand with warm laughter that filled the room. "I'm Tonye Banigo, and I would really love it if you'd allow yourself to be used by God to bless me."

She looked down at their joined hands. "How?"

"Go on a date with me."

This man and his lines. "I thought this was the date."

"Sort of, but I want another one."

"Why?"

"Why not?"

"Why do you want to date me, Tonye?" If his answer made sense, would she go along?

"It's simple, my dear Ibelema. You're easily the most intoxicating woman I've ever met."

She pulled her hand away from him. "Intoxicating" made her sound more exciting than she actually was. "So, you really did say that to Barbara?"

"I did, and I'll say it as many times as I have to until you understand that I'm not playing games here."

Her chest was getting heavier just being in his presence. "Look—" she began.

"You can give me your answer later." He turned toward the counter by the dining table. "But first, do you have anything else you've written that you can show me?"

Ibelema looked at her bag on the counter and back at him. "I don't think you'd—"

"Please, I would love to read your work."

Ibelema's heart raced at his sweet smile. Before Barbara married her husband, she'd always talked about how the more she kept looking at Kay, the more handsome he became.

With a shake of her head, Ibelema pulled out her tablet from her bag. She'd shown most of her stuff to Kay and Daniel, but since Tonye was an actor, he might give good feedback about the other scripts she was working on.

She opened a document and handed him the tablet. "Just let me know when you get bored."

He took the tablet and gave her a slow, patient smile. "I could never get bored with you, Ibe-le-ma."

She threw up her hands in defeat and went to get some snacks while he started reading on the sofa. Every now and then, he would look up at her, his eyes wide. But without saying a word, he would get lost again in the world of her creation.

She kept watching him, waiting for him to say something, though she liked seeing his expressions as he read her work. He seemed to be enjoying himself.

At some point, Ibelema placed a plate of meat pies beside him, and he devoured two of them before looking up from the tablet with a sigh. She had moved to scrub the vomit out of the Persian rug.

"How did you learn to write like this?" Tonye asked.

"You done already?"

He put the tablet down and knelt beside her. "I was going to do that."

"Too late. I want you to keep reading. Did you like it?"

His eyes got big. "You're freaking amazing," he declared, with that infectious smile.

God, he was handsome. And he smelled good too. What was she doing here alone with this man?

He grabbed her free hand, gently tracing the calluses on her fingers. "I saw you play your guitar on YouTube."

"How?" Had he randomly found a video? "You're stalking me now?"

"I wanted to see you."

She chuckled, waiting for him to elaborate. Instead, he just watched her with those intense eyes.

"Why do you keep looking at me like that?" she asked.

"You're beautiful. How else would I look at you?"

Her smile widened, threatening to swallow her face. How could he make her feel so warm inside with just his words? "God, your game, man."

"Corny?"

"God help me," she answered, shaking her head.

"God help me first."

"Why? I'm the one in danger here."

Tonye bent his head to hers, dangerously close. "I'm in trouble too. I'm trying my hardest not to kiss you right now."

She couldn't bring herself to turn away. "What makes you think I would let you?"

Tonye leaned in even closer. "Tell me my sugar, what do you see in my eyes?"

He was too close. She tried to get up but couldn't feel her legs.

"Can't you see how much I want you? That I'm falling in love with you?"

He gazed at her, as if willing her to understand. She couldn't move, couldn't break his spell. He was close enough for his lips to graze hers softly, setting sweet fire razing from her mouth to her thighs. She couldn't think, didn't want to. If it felt this good, why not just let him?

"Tiwa is awake," he whispered, jolting her back to reality.

Ibelema jerked for the baby monitor. Tiwa was crying. As if being chased by her guilt, she bolted up the stairs, thanking God for Tiwa. She really was about to let this man do whatever he wanted to her.

When Ibelema came downstairs with Tiwa, Tonye had a bottle ready, and Tiwa went to him without whining. While Tonye fed Tiwa, Ibelema got some jollof rice from the fridge. She decided she needed something to do—since she couldn't just sit there with him and have to look into his eyes again—so she stir-fried some leftover beef and vegetables.

"This is incredible," Tonye said after a while, chewing his food like he'd never tasted anything that good. He pointed at her feeding Tiwa small cuts of beef. "You'd make a good mother." He grabbed his phone and took a picture of Ibelema feeding Tiwa rice. "So that I can remember you two just as you are right now."

When they finished dinner, they went to the backyard and put Tiwa on the swing. Tonye pushed the swing while Ibelema made funny faces to make Tiwa laugh.

Later, they put Tiwa in her stroller and went for a walk around the neighborhood. They didn't go far, just to the stop sign about two football fields away, and then they headed home because Tiwa was looking sleepy.

"Have you ever been in love?" Tonye asked out of nowhere, as they walked back.

"Maybe," she said, avoiding his gaze. There was a time when she thought she loved Kenneth. "But I think I was more in love with the idea of him and how everyone thought he was perfect for me."

"Sorry," he whispered.

"What about you?" He said he was falling in love with her, but they'd only known each other for a month. Maybe that was a normal thing for him.

"If you asked me before today, I would've said no."

"But something changed today?" The answer hit her before he could answer, and she rolled her eyes. "Right. Another one of your lines."

His eyes were soft. "Real talk, I think I fell in love today."

Before she could reply, Kay's car pulled up behind them in the driveway and veered to the garage. Ibelema and Tonye smiled at each other, a silent understanding that their time together had come to an end.

"When can I see you again?" Tonye half-asked, half-pleaded. He looked at her like his heart would break if she turned him down.

"Soon," she said. "We'll go on another date."

He brightened as if he'd won the lottery. Was this what a man in love looked like? And he was in love—with her?

"I'm so happy right now," he cheered.

Ibelema patted his arm. Maybe he wasn't the only one falling in love.

11

Ibelema entered the café with a guilty smile. Kimani was seated at their table with her green power shake and Ibelema's favorite mango blast smoothie. The cozy café in Sugar Land was one of their favorite spots.

"I feel like it's been ages since you were free," Ibelema teased, as she pulled out her chair.

Kimani frowned. "Yeah, with Thandi starting middle school this fall, I can barely keep up. I'm freaking out."

"The Kimani I know doesn't freak out."

"When you have kids, we'll talk again."

Ibelema sipped her smoothie. "Next comes the teenage hormones and boy drama." Kimani's troubled expression made her laugh. How many diaries had she filled up with the names of random guys she could barely remember now? "And soon she'll be heading off to college."

"College is a scary place."

"Your college not mine. I still can't believe you and Daniel have been tight since way back then."

Kimani shook her head. "We weren't tight back then. He was really cool with..."

"Baron?" Ibelema laughed. "Why do you talk about him like he isn't still around?"

Kimani looked surprised. "Daniel told you?"

Ibelema nodded. She'd read the draft of Daniel's novel based on his past life. All the real names were changed, but Ibelema was able to recognize Kimani from the stories her friend had told her, including the ones about the boy Kimani had crushed on from middle school through college.

"He wrote about everything?" Kimani asked in disbelief.

"Yeah, both you and Sebastian tell what happened from your points of view."

Kimani bobbed her head. "Daniel said Bas told him his side of the story."

"It was amazing. I read the whole thing without stopping once. You've lived one crazy life, Kimani Moore. I'm surprised you told him to write about it."

Kimani's smile was sad. "I think their stories should be told."

"Thandi's parents?"

"Yeah. Maybe one day when she's old enough, she'll read it."

"You should read it too. I think you'll realize some things you've been running away from."

"Like?"

"You and Sebastian."

Kimani flipped her hand as if she was done talking. "Anyway, I saw the news last night. This Ebola stuff is scary. Are your folks worried about it getting to Nigeria?"

Kimani and her interesting pivots. Kimani didn't like talking about Sebastian while her mom couldn't stop talking about Ebola. "Africa's the worst place for Ebola to show up," Ibelema groaned. "All they want to do is pray. It's like prayer has become a cop-out for these politicians."

"Madam Activist," Kimani teased.

"Nigeria is so vexing. There's a wealth of natural resources, and yet talented people are wasting away because of a society that refuses to change. They keep feeding the corruption and Nigerians are suffocating under the weight."

"You're still thinking about moving back home?"

Ibelema hadn't stepped foot in Nigeria since she was a teenager, but the thought crossed her mind every now and then. "Maybe one day, but I have things to do here first."

"Like babysitting with Tonye? Did you guys make out?"

Ibelema choked on the smoothie as the waiter brought their food. Kimani grabbed a handful of Ibelema's fries, then halved her sandwich and put the half on Ibelema's plate.

"That was some reaction," Kimani said with pure delight. "I love it. When are we getting married?"

"You're a joker." And yet, the man kept coming to her mind—a flash here and there of his charming smile, his abs practically carved of marble, or how he looked ridiculously sexy in his reading glasses.

"Is he a believer?" Kimani asked.

Somehow, during their eventful day together, the question never came up. Tonye was definitely a Christian, but being a believer wasn't the same as being a Christian. These days, everyone was a Christian, but only a few were true believers, which was why Kimani had stressed the last word.

"You don't know?" Kimani pressed her.

"Girl, you know some of these brothers are worse than the devil himself."

Kimani laughed. "True. But the way he's got you blushing, are you sure nothing happened?"

Ibelema looked outside the window at the cars zipping along the nearby Hwy 6. "We almost kissed," she mumbled, wincing when Kimani's jaw dropped.

"Seriously, when are we getting married? The IB I know doesn't just kiss anyone."

Ibelema heard herself giggle. It was strange the effect the man had on her. He made her want to do things she'd never thought of doing. After the initial awkwardness on Saturday, she'd found it easy to be around him. He didn't take himself too seriously, and for Tiwa to bond with him that quickly had to mean something.

Kimani tapped the table. "If he's anything like whatshisname, he wouldn't pass the smell test."

"Smell test?" Tonye smelled a little too good, like expensive cologne. But that wasn't what Kimani was talking about.

"I could smell Kenneth's trash self from a mile away," Kimani continued, with a slow roll of her eyes.

Ibelema managed to smile. The fact that she no longer felt sad whenever his name was mentioned meant she was healing. "I was too wrapped up in him to know what he smelled like," she joked.

"Don't be so hard on yourself," Kimani comforted her, in the same patient voice she used when she spoke with her preteen. "God has someone far better for you than Kenneth."

Ibelema's mom had said the same thing, but how could anyone be sure? Kenneth had fooled her, had fooled everyone. Even eagle-eyed Dad didn't see through Kenneth's performance because he looked great on paper, and in person. Only Daniel and Kay had warned her not to trust Kenneth until he actually proposed. But Ibelema thought Kay was annoyed that she was talking to someone other than his best friend. And now, that same Tonye was asking her to date him? Why were men so—what was the word... ridiculous?

"All I'm saying is that Kenneth was the exception, not the rule," Kimani went on. "There are still good guys left, like Daniel and Judah, and if you think this new guy is one of them, give him a chance. Especially since you think he's cute and y'all had a good time this weekend." She winked at Ibelema. "Maybe he'll surprise you."

With the film's schedule and Dad's tax deadline approaching, she didn't have time to start a relationship with a man who would soon return to Nigeria. She couldn't bring herself to look up Tonye on social media because there was no point. He'd already shown her he was different, and there was something so sweet about him that made her want to get close to him. Their conversations were easy and she didn't have to force herself to have fun when she was with him.

"Girl, just let go and let God." Kimani raised her smoothie cup in a toast.

Ibelema tapped cups with her. "Right back at you, girl."

"Ain't nobody looking my way."

"Ma'am? Do I really need to remind you about Sebastian Baron Bailey?"

Kimani pretended to examine her nails. "Who? There's nothing between me and that man."

"Sure." Ibelema chuckled, looking down at her phone vibrating on the table. She fought to keep her face straight. A message from Tonye.

"Who's that?" Kimani leaned forward to sneak a glimpse.

Ibelema snatched up her phone with an innocent smile. "Let go and let God."

12

On Saturday, Silas showed up early to the chapel. He had spent most of the night preparing for the back-to-back scenes. When he'd texted IB to ask her out again on an official date, she had replied that she would have lunch with him only if he nailed the two scenes they were shooting today.

IB was clearly in a good mood. She smiled at him before they started filming, and that smile was still there after the first scene wrapped up. His director looked straight out of a trendy African fashion magazine; fitted blue jeans and purple *ankara* top, her Afro puff resting atop her head like a crown.

As the shoot went on, the scenes flowed so effortlessly that IB didn't stop them once. By noon, they were done filming the heated meeting between the Rev and Pastor Samuel. A loud applause filled the chapel as Silas hugged his co-lead Obadiah.

IB gave Silas a thumbs up from where she stood next to the

camera. In turn, he gave her a dramatic bow, wondering if she would keep her promise. He couldn't remember the last time he'd been so excited by the mere prospect of hanging out with anyone. Since the day they'd watched Tiwa, Silas had to hold back from blowing up her phone. Her last text "See you on Saturday" had left him giddy like a schoolboy ready for Christmas break.

This past week, IB had sent over more of her work for him to read. Her manuscripts flowed like novels, so well-written he could picture the scenes overflowing with unique details that made the dialogue shine. She had a gift for storytelling, but the dialogue was the best part. Her protagonists were likable, yet the villains were on another level. His innocent IB wrote as if she identified more with antagonists than heroes. The character developments and shocking plot twists provoked surprising reactions from Silas, forcing him to reflect on his own humanity. When was the last time he sacrificed everything for someone else?

"Great stuff, Tonye." Efe tapped his arm. "I hope the rest of your day is even more awesome." She winked as if she knew what Ibelema promised him.

Silas fought a laugh. "Thanks, you too." She was adorable, in a little sister kind of way. Efe skirted around him, clearing the path to IB, who miraculously stood alone. Silas met her as she grabbed her duffel bag.

"That was really good," IB said.

He grinned at her. "So...?"

She slung her bag over her shoulder. "What's your plan?"

"I was thinking we could go to one of your favorite spots."

"I'm pretty vanilla, you won't like my favorite spots." She waved at the people leaving the chapel.

"Vanilla? Not a rocky road, mint-chocolate type of woman? What's your favorite cuisine?"

"Vietnamese," she said without hesitation. "And I don't like chocolate. I do love butter pecan, and pistachio, though."

Silas snorted. "You're proving my point. That doesn't seem like something Miss Sweet like Sugar should be eating."

IB sputtered in laughter. "You're a mess."

"Is that good or bad?"

"I haven't made up my mind yet."

"I have."

IB eyed him as if trying to catch his meaning. Somehow, she looked even more beautiful today.

"Anyway, I'm sorry but I have to take a raincheck today." She turned to walk toward the exit. "Can we meet up during the week instead?"

"Why? Did something happen? Or you just changed your mind?" Why did it sound like he was whining?

"I'm not flaking on you. I just forgot I had to do something else today."

"What do you have to do?"

She looked like she was weighing whether to tell him. "I have to go to Austin."

"The capital?" What was she going there for? "And I can't go with you?"

IB paused outside the door to look at him. "Why would you want to go with me?"

"Because you promised we would hang out."

"Promised?" she stuttered. "I wouldn't go that far."

"Are you going to see a guy?"

"Of course not. But even if I was, how is that any of your business?"

He sighed. "If you haven't noticed, I'm trying to get you to fall in love with me."

She blinked, took a step back. "And then what? You're going back to Nigeria." He didn't expect her to say that as she met his eyes. "You haven't thought that far, right?"

"No," he admitted. "But I've decided to take life one day at a time." She chuckled and covered her mouth. "You're so pretty when you laugh. Your eyes get all—"

"Tonye, please."

"Okay. Just let me come with you to Austin."

"You'll be bored."

"I already told you, nothing about Ibelema Pepple could ever be boring."

She waved him off and walked to her car, Silas at her heels. The parking lot had almost cleared out.

"What's in Austin?"

"I'm picking up books for someone," she replied.

"You're driving three hours to pick up books?" Did she come up with that just to avoid hanging out with him?

"She's a widow who can't get around, and wants to donate some rare textbooks her husband left to B4K—"

"B4K?" Silas echoed in disbelief before he burst out laughing. Of course she was involved with Books4Kids.

IB wrinkled her nose in the most adorable way. "Yeah., What's funny?"

"Nothing. Kay put you on to it?"

She nodded. "Right, it was you. You guys started B4K back in law school."

Silas was smiling so wide his cheeks ached. "Now I really have to go with you. I'll even drive." He pointed to his Kia parked in an empty row. "What kind of books are they?"

"Sci-tech mostly."

"Meaning big and heavy. Your ride is—cute."

"Is that your way of insulting my car?"

He crossed the parking lot to his SUV, waving her forward to follow him. He unlocked the car and opened the passenger door.

"I'm a careful driver," he said when IB stalled by the door.

"That's not the issue. You don't have to go all the way to Austin. We can just reschedule the date."

He shook his head. "I've been wanting to see Austin, and if this lady is donating books to our charity, shouldn't I thank her in person?" His chest pounded as he spoke the words. Austin was at least a two-hour trip, so if he could get her to ride with him, they would have five hours of uninterrupted time with traffic. But if she turned him down, who knew when next he would be able to see her outside of the shoot again?

"You're weird," she said, entering the car.

Silas closed the door behind her and ducked into the driver's seat. "Don't worry, I'll even buy you lunch and dinner and snacks on the way."

"I'm the one who should be buying. You're doing me a favor by giving me a ride."

Silas leaned toward her and she moved back against the door. "You don't get it, do you? I have the pleasure of spending the rest of the day with you. So actually, it's really you who's doing me a favor."

Her face softened. "If you put it that way, I guess it's okay then." When Silas rewarded her with a wink, she slapped his arm. "Drive, silly."

Silas playfully rubbed his arm. They were finally getting somewhere.

Five more hours to go. Hopefully, there would be a lot of traffic.

13

Ibelema tucked her fingers under her thighs to stop herself from biting her nails. She couldn't believe she was riding with Tonye so far away from home. To make things worse, he kept messing with her, all flirtatious smiles and longing gazes. When she thought he wasn't looking, she grabbed her phone out of her bag to text Kimani.

"You forgot something?" He drove with one hand, leaning back like a seasoned long-distance driver. "We can still turn back."

They were on I-10 by the Energy Corridor. She could still cook up a story and make him drop her off at Memorial Mall to catch a ride back home. Mrs. Adamson could wait another weekend.

"Oh, nice." Tonye exited the freeway and pulled into a gas station. "I'll get us something to eat."

Before she could protest, he left the car running and hustled into the gas station. Ibelema took out her phone again, her pulse hammering in her ears. What if her mom called while she was on the road? Her parents knew she was going to Austin, but they'd never understand how her solitary adventure had somehow turned into a date.

She'd just shot Kimani another text when the car dashboard started ringing. Tonye had left his phone attached to the charger. "That Lady" appeared on the dashboard.

Who in the world was "That Lady"? Some woman he was messing with? What did she even know about this man to be crossing the state with him? Suddenly irritated, she stared at the windshield as he bounced out of the store with a bright smile and a brown bag in hand.

Tonye entered the car laughing. "You always have your metal bottle with you, so I figured you mostly drink water." He handed her a big bottle of water and cracked open his water bottle.

"Yeah, thanks. I drink a lot of water."

He placed the brown bag on the console between them. "I stumbled on these tacos when I got gas one time. Hands down the best I've ever had. Try the pork, it's wicked spicy."

The tacos smelled so good, her stomach rumbled, reminding her of the quick breakfast of PB&J on toast. She grabbed one of the wrapped tacos. If he was trying to make her relax by feeding her, she wouldn't make it that easy.

"Someone called 'That Lady' called you," she said, unwrapping the foil.

Tonye slung his arm behind her chair and reversed out of the parking spot. "Ah, is that why the car seems much colder than when I left it?"

What was he smiling about? Didn't he have the decency to

feel shame?

"She's no one," Tonye added.

"That's what they all say."

He turned onto the street. "I wouldn't ask you out if there was anyone else, Ibelema. I'm all in with you."

"Then who is she?" No, it wasn't any of her business. Why did it bother her so much? "Actually, it's okay. You really don't have to—"

"That Lady is my mom."

"Your mom?" she repeated, stunned. Why would he call her that?

"I haven't spoken with her in a long time," Tonye explained. "She calls every now and then, hoping I'd pick up one day. I never saved her number, but now that I'm in Texas, it's hard to know who's calling, so I finally saved it." His face went hard as he spoke.

"Where's your mom?" Ibelema asked.

"Right here in Houston."

"And you haven't gone to see her?"

"I didn't come here for her."

Ibelema watched him from the corner of her eye. He looked angry, sad. His mom must have hurt him somehow. "I don't know what happened, but isn't it the right thing to visit her while you're here?"

"She left my dad when I was eight," he scoffed. "Just left with no explanation. She ended up in America, and about ten years ago she started calling me. My dad gave her my number, said I should forgive her, that it wasn't entirely her fault. I didn't even know they'd kept in touch. Can you believe he knew where she was all those years and didn't tell me?"

Ibelema lowered the taco onto her lap. This wasn't some simple mother-son disagreement. She could sense Tonye's deep resentment toward his mom, the woman who abandoned him as a child. Toward his father for keeping him in the dark. She never imagined he was carrying such a burden. The man seemed so self-possessed and well-rounded, but he had grown up without the love of a mother.

"I didn't tell you so you'd feel sorry for me," he said, as if reading her mind. "I just wanted you to know, I guess."

She had many questions, but now wasn't the time to ask. Tonye had told her one of his deepest secrets, which couldn't have been easy to share. His breathing was heavy just from talking. For him to be so vulnerable, he must be serious about her.

"You didn't have to tell me," Ibelema said.

"I did. Now eat your taco, so we can please change the mood."

She smiled at him before taking a bite. Tonye was right—the pork taco was so delicious that she finished it in record time. He offered her another taco. and she ate while laughing at his corny jokes and answering his never-ending questions about Texas. When they pulled into another gas station in Bastrop, just miles away from Austin, she couldn't believe how much time had passed. It was just like how she'd felt hanging out with him at Barb's house.

"I honestly thought you went to an African church," Tonye said, as they pulled out of the gas station. "The worship is the same, there's thunder-fire prayer, you're even hosting a Holy Fire Convention like the churches back home. Fire Mountain Revival. Living Water Conference."

Ibelema couldn't stop laughing. "It's always some dramatic title like Healer Camp Conference. Supernatural Encounter Revival. Forever Changed Convention."

"Those are actually quite good."

"You have a problem with Nigerian Churches?"

"Not as much as you hate on Nigerian movies."

"I don't hate them," she corrected. "I just think they can do better."

"And I think our churches can do better for the communities they benefit from."

"So you think churches are ripping people off."

"We're on our date, can we please talk about something a little less stressful?" Tonye chuckled. "Tell me your stories, Ibelema. Where do they come from?"

Ibelema sipped water from her stainless-steel bottle. He was right—church hypocrisy was at the earliest a fifth date conversation. "From everywhere. Life, church, stories from the news, the scenes just pop up in my head." She handed Tonye's bottle to him, silently noting his big hands and long fingers. If this was a date, why did it feel so normal without all the anxiety of trying to impress a stranger? Then again, he didn't feel like a stranger. He felt safe, but dangerous too.

"How did you convince your parents to let you work on this film?" Tonye asked. "You probably had to pause your nursing thing, right?"

"I'm on a probationary period for this project."

Tonye looked like he had a follow-up question, but he gulped down half of his bottle and put it back in the holder. "Once they see Mountain, they'll realize you're meant to do this."

He definitely didn't know her parents. "The way you talk about this film sometimes. Why are you so confident?"

"It's you I'm confident in," he corrected. "Sure, it would be a sin to waste your God-given talent for drawing blood and giving people sponge baths—no offense to those truly gifted in that area—but you're really good at filmmaking."

The laughter escaped Ibelema's lips before she could reel it in. The life of a nurse was filled with mundane chores most people would never care for, but she actually liked the feeling of helping people—especially the older folk—who couldn't help themselves. That was why she ended up sponsoring an adult daycare after graduation.

Tonye leaned forward in his seat. The GPS showed thirty miles to Austin. "The day I told my dad I was going to be an actor, he kicked me out of his house. I got back at him by using the name Silas, just to piss him off. It worked; he didn't talk to me for months."

"Silas?" His life was so complicated. She really should have googled him.

"Yeah, my middle name." His laugh was awkward. "My dad hated it after she left, so..." His voice drifted off, as if he got caught in another sad memory.

He didn't talk for a while, and she didn't push him either. Kimani once told her that it was important to let men do most of the talking, because they usually revealed more about themselves than they intended to. Tonye was sharing some serious personal details about his family, so why didn't she feel the need to run away? Instead, she wanted to know more.

Tonye blinked at her as if he suddenly remembered where he was. "I'm sorry."

"It's okay. It's not easy to follow your dreams."

"It shouldn't be hard either." His voice took on a blunt edge. "I never understand why parents forget that they made their own mistakes and learned from them, but never allow us to do the same."

Had he read her diary? "They're trying to protect us," Ibelema said, echoing words she told herself whenever her parents got on her case.

"But how can you grow without facing challenges that stretch your faith?"

"Okay, Pastor Banigo." Now he sounded like a seasoned Christian, which answered Kimani's question about his faith.

"When I have a child of my own—preferably more than one—I'll let them make their own mistakes, and just be there for them when they fall. I'll always encourage them to try again, and I'll just have to accept that I'm not God. I can't see or know everything. Or save them from everything."

Ibelema kept her hands on her lap, fighting the sudden urge to hug him. "You'd make a great dad," she offered.

"You think so?"

"Yeah, if you end up doing what you say. But parents often forget what they said."

"How many kids do you want?"

He was changing the topic again. "More than one for sure. Being an only child is a lot."

"You still didn't answer the question. How many?"

Three always seemed like the perfect number. "I wouldn't mind having three."

He nodded. "Three it is. We're having three kids. Nice."

Ibelema heard herself gasp.

"But you're right," Tonye barreled on. "Being an only child is a lot." He held out his right fist to her. "Here's to having more than one child."

Ibelema bumped his fist before she realized what she was doing. "With our significant others," she said quickly, her cheeks warming.

"Of course. And I just happen to be carrying the most significant passenger I've ever driven in my life."

"There's something really wrong with you."

Tonye burst out laughing. "You're so cheeky, Ibelema. It's cute."

She forced back her smile. "Why do you call me that?"

"It's your name, right?"

"Everyone calls me IB, though."

"Yeah, but it's such a beautiful name. I like how it rolls off my tongue. E-be-le-ma."

She couldn't hold back anymore, crossing her arms with an amused shake of her head. "Just drive, you sweet talker."

"Been doing that for two hours. And I'm only being sweet because of you, my sugar." She made a face. "Too much?"

"Cringy." She smacked his arm, her giggles unrestrained.

By the time they got to Austin, Ibelema almost wished they could keep driving. At least they still had the drive back. This drive had been her most entertaining trip in years, narrowly beating out her Big Bend National Park adventure with Kimani and Thandi last summer. She'd never had this much fun with a guy she was interested in. With Kenneth, she was too caught up in being perfect to relax enough to have fun.

They got off the Interstate, and Tonye maneuvered through the busy Austin streets. Mrs. Adamson's house was in the middle of the city, and weekend parking in the afternoon was a nightmare, but he didn't complain. They waited for a slow-moving couple strolling to their car parked near the house. When the pair finally drove off, Tonye effortlessly reversed into the empty spot.

Ibelema gave him two thumbs up. According to Efe, any man who could parallel-park automatically won points for attractiveness. She got out and Tonye followed her on the sidewalk to a brick duplex jammed in between two colorful houses. Ibelema stepped onto the uneven pathway and knocked on the front door.

A short dark-skinned woman opened the door and peered at them through thick tortoiseshell glasses perched on her nose. With gray hair cropped close to her scalp, a simple caftan blouse and a floral skirt, she looked like a sweet grandma from Finders' Village, the adult daycare back in Houston.

"Are you IB?" The woman's kind eyes bounced between Ibelema and Tonye behind her. "I was only expecting one person."

"Sorry for the short notice, Mrs. Adamson. My friend Tonye came to help me pick up the books. He's one of the founders of B4K."

Mrs. Adamson eyed Tonye for a moment and smiled. "I read about you somewhere," she said. "Please come in."

14

His phone rang before he went inside, but Silas silenced the vibration before slipping the phone back into his pocket. Ejiro could wait. Nothing was more important than IB right now.

Stepping inside from the fresh air, Mrs. Adamson's house was a different world. The harsh smell of incense made it hard to breathe, and the house was darkened by heavy curtains. IB was talking to Mrs. Adamson, but the woman kept glancing Silas' way. At first, her eyes seemed guarded, then she was all warmth.

"You remind me of my Bernie," she said, pointing at an array of pictures on the ledge. "My late husband."

Silas studied the old photograph of a younger Mrs. Adamson gazing lovingly at a floppy-haired white man. What could he possibly have in common with a white guy? Maybe it was one of the stages of grief he heard about—trying to associate their loved ones with people and things that weren't necessarily connected to them.

Mrs. Adamson picked up the frame and stared at it as if she'd never noticed it there. "I saw him first, but he'd always say he saw me first. Didn't think much of him except he was the whitest man I'd ever seen." She chuckled. "This was Ghana in the 60s."

"Was it love at first sight?" Silas asked.

"For me, no. But Bernie swore I was the only girl for him. We got married after two dates, and we have been married since...well, were married." The small woman seemed smaller as she hugged the picture frame close to her chest, her silence echoing through the house.

"He must have been a really great guy," Silas said.

"He was the best sort of man." Her face softened with tears. "He loved God, and God loved him. I didn't want to live in America, but it was hard to keep rejecting a man who had such good intentions. Like you coming all the way here with her for my books."

"He's here for B4K," IB emphasized. "One of the founders."

"Sure. And the two of you are just friends, right?" Mrs. Adamson snorted when IB nodded. "Young lady, that's usually how it starts. It's really the best way to build a relationship that will last."

Silas choked on a laugh as IB's eyes went wide as saucers. Mrs. Adamson chuckled with him before turning to IB and winking. "If you like him, don't take too long to make up your mind. Good men aren't that easy to find, y'know?"

IB looked like she wanted to run out the door.

"I've said too much," Mrs. Adamson said, a naughty smile playing at her lips. "The books are this way."

In the study, tall shelves stacked with books lined the walls. In the middle of the room, five large boxes were filled with books.

"I'm glad you came," IB said as Silas crouched to lift a box of books from the floor.

He adjusted his glasses. She really did have the prettiest smile. It curved her soft lips and rounded her cheeks, and the light danced in her coffee-brown eyes.

"I knew you'd need me." He carried the first box outside to the car. IB offered to lift one of the boxes, but Mrs. Adamson vetoed her.

"You have to let men be men," the woman scolded her. "Let him show you why you should choose him." She nudged IB. "In the end, it's not them who choose us. It's us who choose them."

Silas took the last box and made one more trip outside. When he got back, IB was nodding at Mrs. Adamson, jerking when she noticed him enter the room. IB said goodbye and hurried out, pulling Silas behind her.

"Hope it all works out," Mrs. Adamson called from the door.

As they drove away from the woman's house, Silas watched IB with concern. She was too quiet. "You okay?"

She offered him a sad smile. "I can't imagine how she's feeling. All those years of being with one person, then one day he's gone. It would be hard to keep going."

"Yeah, usually women last longer than men do when they lose their spouses." His grandmother had lived more than twenty years after his grandfather passed.

"Or the men just get a younger woman. Would you remarry if you lost your wife?"

It sounded like a trick question. "I guess it depends on how close we were. If I loved her fiercely enough."

IB's eyes went soft. "Sometimes you sound like a song."

"I'm an actor, remember?"

"Right...and what does fierce love look like to you, Tonye

Banigo?"

He faced the red traffic light. "I wouldn't know."

"Maybe like Mrs. Adamson and Bernie. She definitely felt like she was the only one for him, and he was her person." IB looked out the window. "Maybe only non-Nigerians have that kind of love. My parents met through a friend and just figured they should marry since they had a lot in common."

Silas couldn't see her face. Was the Adamson's story the sort of love IB dreamed about?

"I guess love happens in different ways," she went on. "The beginning isn't as important as the middle, or the mundane of doing life together...what?"

He shook his head. "Nothing."

"We're going to be in the car for a while."

"Then we need to find something to eat." Silas looked around and didn't recognize driving through this area. He grabbed his phone for directions.

IB touched his hand. "Let's just get something from a food truck. Turn this way."

He ignored the heat on his hand. "You went to school here, right?" The big university was down the road.

"Nope, Barb did. I went to A&M but would come down here for ASA week and other stuff. Barb was the president. We used to go to Sixth Street." She pointed ahead to an open lot sandwiched between buildings. The area was packed with food trucks and hundreds of people.

Silas made a U-turn at the light. Kay had told him about Barbara's college adventures. "Somehow that doesn't make sense. You at a club? I don't see it. Maybe some indie or jazz lounge, or hanging out in the library till they kicked you out."

IB giggled. He expected her to be a little offended. "I did all of that," she said. "But dancing is my guilty pleasure when I go to a fun party. That's one of the reasons I love Kimani. We both love to dance and cut up when we're out. I just haven't been to a club since I pivoted."

"Pivoted," Silas tried the word on his tongue. "Is that another word for saved?"

"Yeah, a word much abused."

The image of IB dancing in her church popped into his head. "Clubs are noisy and sweaty. You're not missing anything."

"I know. Not to mention the random creeps. You may need to park in the garage. Street parking is crazy here."

He pulled to the side of the road. "Wait here. I'll park and come find you."

IB climbed out of the car. "Call me when you get here. I'll stand by this sign."

Silas drove to the packed garage, where it took an irritating amount of time to find a parking spot. Still, he was happy that he'd managed to stretch out the day with IB. He finally found an empty spot on the fourth level and hurried back down. Cars zipped past as he waited at the streetlight. She was hard to miss, her slender shapely figure filling up her purple *ankara* top and snug blue jeans.

Two men stepped to her while she was focused on her phone, and her smile quickly faded into a frown. IB turned away, waving her phone as if to dismiss them, but they circled her, checking her out. These were the sort of guys who lurked around clubs, waiting for a girl to be alone.

The walk sign flashed and Silas jogged up the crosswalk. Why did he have to park so far away?

"I'm waiting for someone," he heard IB say.

The guys hedged IB in, and the shorter one reached for her

butt. He didn't make contact because Silas grabbed the man's hand and dragged him away from IB.

"Step away from her or I'll break his arm," Silas warned the taller guy. He'd learned a thing or two from the stunt guys in his action movies.

IB whirled in his direction, eyes frantic. "What are you doing?"

The short guy struggled to free his hand twisted behind his back, and his friend glared at Silas. "Are you mad? Let him go. You can't do that."

Silas tightened his grip on the man's wrist.

"Tonye, there's a cop looking this way," IB pleaded. "Just let him go."

"Why didn't the cop see them earlier?" Silas barked, twisting the pervert's arm with so much force that the man groaned. "Keep your slimy hands to yourself."

"Tonye, please. It's not that big of a deal."

"Just let go and we'll dip," the tall guy said, eyes darting behind Silas.

The officer was looking their way. People had started to gather around them. Reluctantly, Silas released the man's arm, and the two men scurried off. IB grabbed Silas's hand and they blended into the crowd.

"You didn't have to do that," she said. "I was about to pull out pepper spray."

He looked back, scanning the crowd for the men. "Does that happen often?"

IB pulled him to a food truck that served pho. "I haven't used it once since Barb gave it to me. Church guys are way more careful. And I don't look like Barb."

"Meaning?"

IB moved forward in the line of people. "Barb's a typical Naija babe; perfect hourglass shape that every guy likes. Me, my best asset is my smile." She flashed him her signature smile, probably as proof.

Silas knew she was trying to lighten the mood. "What are you talking about? You're freaking gorgeous. Why do you think guys are always looking at you?"

The couple in front of them laughed, and IB elbowed Silas in his side.

"It's true." He pointed at two men standing in another line across from them. "They were literally just checking you out right now."

"Stop." IB turned to look at the two guys, and they shrugged as if to say "Guilty."

Silas laughed at the horror on her face. "You have many asssssets," he joked and dodged her blows. "Trust me. Objectively speaking, you're a very beautiful woman."

She squinted at him. "Just objectively speaking?"

"I would say the same thing even if I had no skin in this game."

"That sounded wrong on many levels."

He took in her smooth caramel skin and full mouth. "You have no idea the things I would do to you, Ibelema."

"Jesus. Get behind me, Satan."

He laughed. "Next up, butter pecan ice cream for dessert."

After they got their Vietnamese food, they strolled around and found an ice creamery, where IB ordered a vanilla-pecan fusion with a hint of pistachio. Away from the packed square, they sat on a bench near the road.

They slurped noodles while people-watching, and IB made up stories about the couples that passed by. When he wasn't choking with laughter at her detailed characterizations, Silas gazed at IB in awed silence. He couldn't remember when last he'd eaten a simple meal with a woman that didn't involve awkward conversation. Hanging out with IB felt easy...too easy at times. Her honesty and sense of humor were disarming. She wasn't a woman who played games, probably because she didn't know how to play them. And to make it sweeter, she was wonderful to look at. How could a woman this beautiful be so unaware of the effect she had on men?

With a thoughtful smile, IB tilted her head to the side. A group of people were dancing nearby to a lovely melody that Silas wasn't familiar with. The falling sun cast a soft light behind her. "I love that song," she crooned.

"You're a songbird," he whispered.

Her eyes lit up. "I like that. Songbird." She bobbed her head. "Music has helped me through many hard times. Some songs are like old friends, y'know?"

This was the perfect chance. "Then dance with me."

"Yeah, right." She blinked at him. "Wait, you mean here?"

Setting his finished bowl to the side, he wiped his hands on his jeans, stood to his feet, and offered her his hand. "I've been waiting to dance with you."

Her smile spread wide across her face as she followed suit. When IB put her hand in his, a jolt of electricity shocked up his arm.

"What do you think this is, a rom-com?"

Silas kissed the back of her palm, and water hit his cheek. He looked up to see more drops of rain falling, took off his glasses and put them in his pocket. When did the clouds get dark?

IB held a hand over her head as the rain fell harder like cool pellets on their faces. Thunder cracked the sky, and people around them bolted to their cars.

"This is fun," IB cried, seemingly unbothered by the downpour. No shrieking over her hair, makeup, or designer clothes getting messed up. Instead, she was like an excited schoolgirl. If Silas didn't know better, he'd guess she was about to start jumping in puddles.

He blinked back the trickle at the corner of his eyes. How could all these wonderful things be rolled up into one person? How was he supposed to leave her and go back to Nigeria?

"I thought you wanted to dance," she cried, spinning in the rain.

His heart wanted to stay there and watch her, but they were getting drenched, and the garage was several blocks away. People were taking shelter underneath the storefronts. He grabbed her hand and spun her around before breaking into a half-jog, half-dance toward a nearby record store. IB's eyes glittered, and her infectious laugh rang out despite being soaking wet. She looked like she was having the best time. And when she turned that sweet soft smile his way, Silas knew she was telling him how she felt. She liked him, too.

"Let's run for it," IB said.

He wanted to kiss her, right there in the rain, but she tugged his arm. He glanced at her feet; sneakers, not heels. "I'll carry you," he offered. "That would make for a story we can tell our kids."

With the cheekiest smile, IB broke into a jog again. It took Silas a moment before he realized she was getting a head start to the garage. He caught up to her easily and grabbed her hand. Under the steady stream of the rain, she clung to him, and his heart thundered against his ribs, hopelessly in love.

"I like this story better," she teases, pulling him down the street.

15

The lights flashed from every corner as the event photographers paced the room, and Silas kept turning his face to avoid the cameras. On the stage, the Global Partners President called out the first award.

Silas glanced at IB sitting beside him at the round table. He'd asked her to attend the gala with him, and she'd surprised him by agreeing. When Kay initially mentioned the fundraiser, he didn't say that the gala's guest list included local politicians and news celebrities. Two tables away, Silas recognized a well-known Houston rapper who toured Nigeria last year.

"Even our congresswoman is here," an excited Barbara informed them.

"No wonder the list was so tight," Kay said. They'd pulled strings to get IB into the gala at the last moment.

IB smiled at Silas, and heat passed between them when their

eyes met. When they got back from Austin, they'd shared an awkward hug in the church lot before she rushed off. Since then, the carefree Ibelema from their road trip was gone. Probably still trying to sort out her feelings for him.

The crowd applauded as the first award was called for Global Partners Ambassadors, North America. An elderly Caucasian lady hobbled up to the stage to receive the honors. Her name and picture flashed on the screen behind the stage. She was the founder of an American NGO.

The next award was for one of the GP Ambassadors in South Asia. A photographer stopped at their table and Silas instinctively turned away.

Kay chuckled. "It amazes me how someone who hates cameras can be an actor. Maybe you should consider a career change."

"Like what?" Barbara asked. "A politician?"

"Exactly," Kay said, no hint of teasing in his voice. "Nigerian senators don't get harassed as much either, y'know."

"Tonye? A senator?" IB mumbled.

"Stop it," Silas told Kay, the idea too silly to entertain.

"Think of all the work you're doing back home," Kay went on. "B4K, CPC, flood rescue, Makoko. Come on, man. You're meant for this."

"Aren't you forgetting what they think of me right now?" Silas whispered, and his stomach turned. Why would Kay bring it up when IB was here? IB smiled at him as if she thought him being a senator was a good idea.

Two familiar faces appeared on the giant screen behind the stage.

"Global Partners Ambassadors, Africa," the president called over the mic, and their names flashed on the screen. "Tonye

Banigo and Kay Ojo."

Kay kissed Barbara full on the lips and beamed at Silas. "Let's go, partner."

Silas got up in a daze. IB and Barbara were clapping, and the whole room was looking at them. So this was why Kay had insisted he come. Did Kay think he was exaggerating when he said Maxwell Johnson was out to get him?

"Why didn't you tell me?" Silas hissed.

"You'd never come if I did." Kay led Silas to the stage amidst the roaring applause. People reached out for handshakes on their way. An older gentleman even bear-hugged the two of them.

"They chose us for the whole of Africa?" Silas asked, his throat tight.

"Congrats." Kay clapped Silas on the back. "You're the best man I know and you deserve this. I'm proud of you."

Silas didn't know how he made it to the stage with the blinding lights. He shook hands with three GP board members, and when a light flashed too close to his face, he frowned at the photographer. Kay placed a hand on his shoulder.

"Just keep smiling," Kay warned through his ever-ready photo smile. "IB is watching."

"What do you take me for?" Silas mumbled.

Kay took the plaque from the GP president and held it high, posing for another photo before handing Silas the plaque. "Thank you so much for this honor," Kay began.

As Kay talked, Silas looked out to the crowd where IB sat holding Tiwa on her lap. His goddaughter was decked out in a green frilly dress with a pink bow. But it was IB who stole the show. She was always beautiful, but tonight, in her fitted gown with one exposed shoulder, and natural hair braided down her back, IB was a total knockout.

Silas exhaled a ragged breath. It was getting harder and harder to think about anything else when she was around.

Kay wrapped up his speech, and a woman led them off the stage. Silas thought they were heading back to their seats, but the woman gestured backstage, probably to take more pictures.

His eyes scanned the crowd in search of Ibelema, but what he saw made him stop so abruptly in his tracks that Kay bumped into him. Silas squinted across the hall. "You gotta be kidding me," he muttered.

"What's going on?" Kay asked, pulling him across the stage.

Silas moved backstage and to the side, hidden but still in view of their table. Yeah, it was him. The man with the scar on his right cheek.

"What are you looking at?" Kay peeked from behind the backstage wall. The woman who led them from the stage stood waiting for them.

"That guy I told you followed me from the airport to my hotel? He's here."

"What do you mean he's here?"

"Look, he's sitting over there. Two tables behind IB."

"Behind Tiwa?"

Silas made to go down the stage, but Kay held him back. When did the man get there? He wasn't at that table before they left for the stage.

"That will draw too much attention," Kay said. "If it's really him, we gotta come up on him from behind."

Before Silas knew it, a security guard approached the scarred man at his table and gestured for him to get up. The man looked the guard up and down but made no move to stand, so the guard grabbed him by the arm. As the people closest to their table whispered back and forth about the tension, the intruder yanked his hand away. The guard spoke to him in a hushed tone, and seconds later, the scarred man stormed toward the exit with security behind him. IB and Barbara didn't seem to notice a thing.

Silas hustled past a throng of people backstage. "I have to talk to him."

"He clearly knew you would be here," Kay said. "What's he trying to do?"

"Sorry, I ended up dragging you guys into this."

"No, it's on me, man. I shouldn't have made you come."

Less than a minute later, they found the exit. Outside the lobby, the man with the scar was talking to the security guard and another guy in a black suit. As Silas stepped out of the building, the man looked their way, and his face changed, shoving the guard aside to charge at Silas.

In panic, Silas backed away toward the building, but instantly realized that running was the worst thing he could do if the man was actually carrying a gun. He turned to find the stalker swinging at him, and dodged the blow, not fast enough. He felt a sting on his cheek as the blade scraped his skin and blew past his face. Someone screamed behind him. He didn't have time to look to see who.

"You thought you could run away from Mr. Johnson," the man growled, lunging again at Silas. Kay suddenly appeared behind the man and kicked him in the back of his knees, which made him stumble.

That was the opening Silas needed. He launched a right hook and smashed the man's face with his fist. The man fell and his back slammed the ground as the knife clattered across the concrete. When the dazed man tried to get up, Silas kicked his head like he was shooting for goal. The man dropped again and the back of his head hit the ground.

The two guards rushed to pin the man down, but he lay there eerily still. Lights flashed from the parking lot, and two police cars raced over. Silas turned to go back into the building. He froze and Kay grabbed his arm. IB stood by the door to the lobby with Tiwa in her arms.

"We have to stay here," Kay said. "If we leave, it'll look more suspicious."

IB watched them with confused eyes before hurrying back to the hall.

Three police officers surrounded the man and the guards pointed at Silas and Kay. If the guards heard what the man said before trying to stab Silas, the police would have questions for him. What would he tell them—that a thug from Nigeria tried to kill him? Was this what his life had become, always looking over his shoulder? And now he'd even dragged Kay's family into his mess.

Back in the building, at least a dozen people stood in the lobby staring out at them, but IB wasn't among them. What was she thinking right now? Any explanation other than the whole truth wouldn't make sense to her. He couldn't bring her into his drama too. He couldn't keep living like this. If Maxwell Johnson wanted to kill him, he had to go back home and face the music.

With his mind made up, Silas turned to face the police officers walking toward him. No matter what, he couldn't stay in Houston anymore.

16

Ibelema hummed a tune as her fingers lightly strummed her guitar. Music always helped to calm the war in her mind. Last night, she couldn't sleep, and when she closed her eyes to pray, she finally asked the "Tonye" question because she couldn't ignore him any longer.

With or without her consent, her mind kept replaying parts of their Austin trip. On their way back, Tonye blasted the heat until their clothes dried enough to be a little comfortable for the ride. They laughed the whole way and got to Houston after 9 p.m. She'd looked forward to Tonye trying to kiss her again, but he didn't, so when he invited her to his gala, she had jumped at the opportunity to spend more time with him.

Now, she was more confused. She put down her guitar and started to type a reply to Tonye on her phone, then stopped mid-sentence and went to her desk. She didn't want to think about what happened at the gala. His text didn't explain anything. He'd only asked how she was doing. And in the days since the gala, their texts had dwindled. It was awkward talking to him when he didn't want to talk about what she wanted to talk about.

Sighing, Ibelema opened the video files Michael sent over. With less than a month before the submission deadline, they needed to find video editing professionals.

She came across footage of Tonye and Chanel talking in the park, the first scene Tonye shot, and Ibelema still couldn't believe the chemistry between him and her cast from day one. Both Chanel and Efe liked hanging around Tonye because he treated them like his little sisters.

Ibelema replayed the poignant scene which captured the essence of a neglected daughter hanging out with her famous father, the illegitimate daughter whom the Rev hadn't seen in years because he lived in Nigeria and she attended college in Texas.

Had Chanel told Tonye about the problem in the church? What sort of advice would he give her? She suddenly felt the urge to hear his voice and laughed at the silliness of it. Tonye wasn't the sort of man she ever imagined marrying. She wanted a low-key guy, not one used to attention. Just watching the footage reminded her how comfortable he was around women.

With Tonye still on her mind, Ibelema pulled up the Books4Kids website. The About page featured a brief biography of college mates Kay Ojo and Tonye Banigo, founders of the charity for underprivileged school kids. A picture showed the two of them in their university days, surrounded by beaming children. How come she'd never paid attention to Kay's friend before? He looked so cute without his glasses.

Her fingers hovered over the keyboard. She had to know.

She googled 'Tonye Banigo Instagram.' Several accounts popped up., but none of them were his. In one of the pictures, a clean-shaven guy who looked a lot like Tonye posed with sunglasses, his white shirt teasing a muscular chest and ripped abs. The typical Nollywood star, complete with designer labels and an unhealthy abundance of arrogance to match.

Silas Harry at an Award ceremony, the caption read.

Silas. That was the name Tonye went by, but how could this Silas be her Tonye? It was like Clark Kent vs. Superman, but in this case, she actually preferred Clark Kent. Unlike Tonye, Silas wasn't wearing glasses, and his shirt was a size smaller than anything Tonye would wear. How could two sides of the same man be so different?

An email notification flashed on the screen, interrupting her internet stalking. It was from Shoot Me Studios.

"Dear Ibelema," she read aloud. "We're a video production crew looking to diversify our clientele. We heard about your indie film and would love to help get your film ready for the TIFF Festival. Please check out our website for what we can offer. This is not spam—"

Ibelema reported the email as spam and lay her head on the desk. These scammers were getting too bold. It almost felt as if life was laughing at her. What if her dad was right and her filmmaking dream was merely a distraction? Was she disguising her disappointment with life by pouring everything into this film? What would she do once the festival was over and nothing came of it?

"Throw me a bone here," she whispered. "If you don't want me to do this, just tell me. Don't send help if this isn't what you want for me."

Ibelema picked up her guitar again and started messing

around, not playing any song in particular. Before she knew it, she was singing and crying, feeling like a weight was being carried away from her.

Someone knocked on her door, and she scrambled to wipe her eyes. She couldn't even get some privacy at her age.

"Come in," she muttered.

Her mom peeked in through the crack in the door. "Your daddy wants you. He's in his office." She said nothing more, which meant it had to be serious.

Ibelema washed her face and said a prayer before going downstairs. She marched into the home office, ready for battle as she sat across her dad at his desk. These conversations were getting tougher, especially since she didn't have much to report.

When he finally looked up from his laptop, she felt like one of his employees about to get the Pere Pepple treatment. He gave her the no-nonsense frown he often threw the junior accountants and bookkeepers on his staff during the stressful tax season.

Ibelema shifted in her seat, hands folded on her lap. "There's only a couple more scenes to film," she said, already knowing why he'd called her down. "And we're shopping for editors to put everything together."

He frowned. "Aren't you cutting it too close to the submission deadline?"

For someone who wanted her to focus on nursing, Dad seemed a little too concerned about the film. "Everyone has stuff going on, and they're doing it for free, so I have to take what I can get from them."

Dad's eyes softened. Was he smiling? "You have good friends."

"Yeah, I'm grateful for all of them."

The softness instantly morphed into a stern gaze.

"Remember our agreement. Once tax season is over, we're going to sit down and come up with a plan of action. No more aimless days of waking up and coming back whenever."

Ibelema bit her lip. He was always making plans for her, and she was expected to follow him without argument. That was her duty as the only daughter of a traditional Nigerian man, who refused to understand that the times had changed.

"You're spending too much time outside the house. Just because we didn't say anything about you going to Austin and coming back late doesn't mean I approve."

"Dad, I was volunteering, I can't help that it took longer than expected." She never told them about Tonye coming along. Why add fuel to the fire?

He stared at her until she couldn't look at him anymore. "Don't get smart with me."

She considered walking out of the room. At what age would he stop talking to her like this? Would the time ever come when he would acknowledge her as an adult with the common sense to make her own decisions? Maybe not. As long as she was in his house, he could treat her this way. Still, it would break Mom's heart if she left home. The only way her parents would let her go without any drama was if she moved out because she was getting married.

"You know I don't like saying this, but your mates are progressing and getting promoted." Dad sighed, like a man tired of talking. He leaned back in his chair and closed his eyes. "It's okay. You can go."

The instant Ibelema closed the door behind her, she released a deep breath. Her mom and Aunty Osagie were eating in the dining room, reliving a wedding from the weekend. Aunty Osagie waved at Ibelema to join them at the table.

"I heard you were at that international gala a few days ago," Aunty said.

"It was that big?" Mom asked. "Barbara invited her."

"It was big o," Aunty replied. "Some madman tried to stab the congresswoman—"

"Jesus," Mom cried.

"The worst part is he's Nigerian."

"Christ. Why are our people now being involved in things like this?"

"The person who stopped him was Nigerian too, one of your husband's people." Aunty turned to Ibelema. "Did you see what happened?"

"Not really." Ibelema still didn't fully understand what happened either. She saw Tonye get attacked, then beat the crap out of the guy who jumped him. As she had rushed back to the hall to tell Barbara, several high-profile guests were being escorted out of the gala. The security blocked the exit so no one else could leave until half an hour later. When they finally got outside, the women didn't see Kay or Tonye, but Kay texted Barbara to take Tiwa home because he and Tonye were staying behind to answer questions. The next day, the news reported that the congresswoman was nearly assassinated by a Nigerian hitman with ties to the media mogul, Maxwell Johnson. The whole thing made no sense. If the man was after the congresswoman, why did he attack Tonye like he meant to kill him?

"Anyway," Aunty waved off the drama, "I heard you looked beautiful. Someone sent a number for you."

Ibelema frowned at the knowing looks the sisters shared. "What number?"

"Mrs. Peters said her nephew just moved down here from Germany and sent me his picture. Want to see?" She was already pulling out her phone.

"For what?" Ibelema rolled her eyes at the picture of a corny-looking guy wearing a green suit.

"This bush girl." Aunty laughed. "For a date. Just look at his muscles swelling out. He's the type you girls like these days now, *abi*? Look well, Ibelema."

She was done looking. Tonye was way better looking. "Not interested."

"Ibelema," Mom chided. "You didn't even hear her out."

"He's a doctor—" Aunty went on.

Ibelema pulled out her ringing phone from her jeans pocket. "I have to take this." She hurried up the stairs to her room.

"Are you busy?" Barbara asked, on the phone. "I need a favor." Tiwa was wailing in the background, and Barbara sounded on the verge of tears. "Can you please come over?"

Ibelema felt a chill spread over her. For months after giving birth, Barbara had experienced postpartum depression, and since then, the symptoms would reappear every now and then. It had been a while since she'd gotten a call like this, but she knew exactly what to do.

"I'm on my way."

17

Silas ripped the sheets from a roll of tissue paper and blew his nose. As usual, there was nothing interesting to watch on TV. He flipped channels until he saw a group of people singing together like a choir.

Listening to the lyrics, he realized it was a Christian song. He tried to change the channel, but the button didn't work, and he knocked the remote on his palm. His phone rang beside him. Dad. Almost two months since their last chat, he still wasn't ready to talk.

When his phone stopped ringing, Silas scrolled to his messages with IB. He hadn't heard her voice since the gala. He'd texted her, but because she was waiting for him to explain what happened that night, all of her responses sounded dry. He wanted to explain, but didn't know where to start. It probably didn't matter anymore at this point. She'd probably found out about the scandal after reading the nasty stories about him online.

His phone rang again. His dad never called back-to-back. He snatched the phone before he could change his mind.

"Tonye," Dad cried in a relieved tone. "Thank God. You're in America, I saw the news."

The news had reached Nigeria already? "Yeah, I'm good, Dad."

"Why didn't you tell me you were leaving?" Dad asked. "No, that's my fault. I'm sorry, son, for how everything's gone between us."

Silas took a deep breath, his chest aching at the words he had longed to hear. He'd thought he would be angry whenever he finally got around to speaking to his dad, but now, it felt like he was putting down a weight he had been carrying for months.

"You sound sick. It's okay, you don't have to tell me anything. I'm just glad you're safe."

"Sorry. I should've called you back." Silas swiped a falling tear from his cheek. Why didn't he call him? Was he that ashamed of who he'd become? Was that why he couldn't tell IB the truth?

"My dear son, I love you more than anything. You know that, right?"

Silas placed the tissue over his runny nose. A salty tear rolled into his mouth. His chest felt so tight he could barely breathe.

"Yeah," he managed to say.

"And you know I believe you? You would never do what they're accusing you of."

All Silas could do was nod as his tears flowed freely. Where was all this emotion coming from?

"That's why you need to come back home and fix this. With that genius brain of yours, you're letting some ignoramus old riffraff drag you into their mud." His voice was thick with righteous indignation. "Your name is Datonye: God's gift. That's why I was angry with you. I didn't name you Datonye for you to be following every Tom, Dick and Harry's plan for your life. You're bigger than what you've been doing. I always thought you would go into politics and help change this country. You're God's gift to me. To Nigeria."

"God? Wasn't it God who put me in this situation?" Silas punched the couch cushions, silently cursing every journalist publishing lies against him, lies that IB would read and believe.

"Yes, God allowed it to happen. But do you know why, Tonye? You allowed it to happen first. You allowed all these strange things into your life, to the point that there's no room for God. All the rooms in your heart are already filled up with things that are only holding you back."

Silas watched the TV with the animated choir lifting their hands in passionate worship on the screen. No room for God? Was that why God wasn't helping him? Growing up, Dad always said that too many people wanted God to lead them but weren't actually willing to be led. "You can't expect the king to help you," his sage dad would say, "if you're not the king's friend. Or if you aren't serious about obeying the king's rules."

"Are you saying that me being an actor is disobeying God?"

Dad was quiet for a moment. "What I know is that you being an actor has moved you further away from God. Can you honestly say that isn't true?"

No, he couldn't. He'd never been the most spiritual guy, but in years past, he did feel like he and God had an understanding of sorts. In a way, maybe his life had always revolved around God. After his mother left, he had spent countless hours with his dad's church friends. The women at church would feed him and he hung out with their kids while Dad was at work. The charity initiatives he was now involved in were directly influenced by the lessons those women instilled in him: everyone had a purpose, but each one needed to find themselves before they could live their most fulfilling lives.

"Dad, I—" It was the best excuse to hang up. Silas needed answers, and fast. He didn't have the luxury to be thinking about God and his purpose right now. "Ejiro is calling me. I'll call you back later."

"Ejiro?" Dad shouted. "That snake? Tonye, one of my investigators discovered something about Ejiro you should know."

A shiver curled up his back. "You had someone follow Ejiro?"

"Why not?" he countered, totally ignoring the deliberate accusatory tone in Silas' voice. "I never understood how that school dropout became your agent, so yes, I checked on him. And it turns out he's involved in all this. How do you think the camera knew to be right outside your house waiting for you? It was Ejiro who told them."

Silas swallowed the mucus choking his throat. "W—Why would he do that?"

"That conniving snake has been dancing on your head, having meetings with that old fool Johnson, cutting deals behind your back. He owes some bad people a lot of money."

Ejiro had always introduced Silas to sketchy women and suggested that a bad-boy image would help his career. That night, he'd been waiting at home for Ejiro when that Jezebel Jeanie appeared. How else would she know where to find him? Had Ejiro set him up?

"Was he working with Jeanie Johnson?" Silas asked.

Dad laughed. "Well, we should hear all about it on her upcoming exclusive with—"

"Jeanie is giving an interview?"

"You didn't hear? Why do you think I'm telling you to come back? The tide is turning. Now's the time to sue the devil out of them."

Silas sat on the edge of the couch, cradling his head in his hands. "I didn't hear anything."

"After your heroism in Houston, things have gotten bad for Johnson. No one knows where he is, but the government people are after him because they don't want any bad blood with America. It's only a matter of time before America finds him. You don't go after one of their own and not—"

"But that's not what hap—"

"Tonye!" Dad snapped. "That is what happened. They're reporting that Johnson was involved in shady business deals that the American congresswoman was rallying against. He lost a lot of money because of her, so he was trying to send a message in front of her colleagues."

How in the world had the story changed to that? When the police finally talked to them outside the gala, the security guards had already spun a different narrative to the police. Apparently, the guards heard the man mumble "Mr. Johnson," and yelled the congresswoman's name as the target before Silas just happened to get in his way. Both Kay and Silas only needed to agree with the story the cops laid out for them, and Kay had eagerly planted the seed that Mr. Johnson was most likely the infamous Maxwell Johnson.

As they drove home that night, Kay explained that the guards probably lied because naming the congresswoman as the target meant the guards automatically became heroes for stopping an assassination instead of some random stabbing.

"Do you understand?" Dad asked. "Yes, God allowed all of

this to happen, but also made a way out for you. It's time to clear your name, son. The media has turned in your favor, and everyone's wondering if Johnson set you up to get you out of the way. They're saying you have proof of his shady dealings. So as soon as you get back here, you'll do an in-depth interview and we'll sue Johnson and his agency."

After that declaration of war, his dad said goodbye and hung up.

Silas slid off the couch and onto the fluffy carpet, staring blankly at the rotating blades of the ceiling fan turn as the singers on TV started another song in the background. A moment that should have ended his life was somehow turning out for his good, just like the verse Dad used to quote back in the day.

He fumbled for the remote and turned up the volume. The music was calming, as if someone was in the house with him. He glanced around just to make sure, but he remembered the feeling. He hadn't felt it in a long time.

His old man was right. Becoming an actor had pulled him away from God. But did that mean his acting career had been a mistake? As an actor, he'd been empowered to do a lot of good, to reach places and people he couldn't as a lawyer. But what good did that do him? Ejiro of all people had betrayed him.

Silas turned on his side to face the TV. Watching the singers, he imagined IB among them, dancing around the stage. This morning, he'd noticed it for the first time: the silence. He had never minded being alone, but now, whenever he wasn't with her, he felt suffocated by the silence in a way he couldn't explain.

It was surrounding him even now. His breaths came faster, and he opened his mouth to breathe. IB had shown up in his life and made everything come alive. He'd forgotten how it felt to wake up every day and have something to look forward to, a hope that life had more to offer than he could ever imagine.

"Please, help me," he whispered into the silence. He wanted to see her, to tell her everything, to make her understand and love him in spite of his mistakes.

"I will change." He couldn't move forward without her. He couldn't stay in Houston, but he didn't want to go back home if it meant living without her.

"Just show me what to do. Give me a sign." Silas knelt beside the sofa and buried his face in the pillow. He opened his mouth, but he didn't know what else to say.

The doorbell rang.

18

Ibelema got out of her car outside the faded brick bungalow where Tonye's Kia was parked in the driveway. She grabbed the cooler and scanned the quiet neighborhood, noting the nearest house far away. For a moment, she thought the neighbor's front door opened, but no one came out.

After rushing to Barbara's house, Ibelema had found there was no real emergency. Tiwa and her parents were sick, so Barbara begged Ibelema to take the pepper soup she'd cooked over to Tonye, who sounded worse than all of them when Kay had talked to him on the phone.

Ibelema felt bad that she hadn't texted him or called him, but if Tonye was sick, Barbara's fire pepper soup would help him feel better. Even if she was unsure of where they stood, she still wanted to see him. She needed to know what happened the night of the gala. If they were going to move forward with whatever this was, he owed her an explanation.

The sound of her own knocking on Tonye's door made her heart jump. She should have texted to let him know she was coming.

The door cracked open and Tonye's face appeared. He squinted from behind his glasses, then his face exploded into a bright smile she didn't expect.

"You're actually here," he said, swinging the door wide open.

Was he hoping she would come? That was sweet. Other than the nasal lilt to his deep voice, he didn't look sick. She noticed a small cut on his cheek, most likely from the attack. She couldn't believe he had fended off a man with a knife.

Ibelema lifted the cooler in explanation. "Special delivery from Barbara."

He didn't bother looking at the cooler. "You didn't have to."

"I just came to drop it off." The way Tonye was gazing at her, it was probably better to hand him the soup and go home. When she tried to hand him the cooler, he didn't reach for it.

"You can't just come here and not come in," he said.

Ibelema felt her head nod, and her feet moved against her better sense. She stopped at the doorway and looked up at his warm eyes. Something about the moment felt final, like if she took one more step into his world, she'd never be able to go back to how she was now.

Tonye pulled her in and closed the door behind him. "Want something to drink? I have juice, tea, water."

"I'm fine." The open floor house was clean and airy, and a peninsula counter separated the living room from the kitchen. She placed the cooler of soup on the counter and watched him guzzle down a bottle of water.

"Are you okay?"

He cleared his throat. "Yeah, why?"

How could he look this handsome even when he was sick? "You don't look sick. Is it the flu?"

"I don't know. You expected me to be laid out on the couch?" He chuckled. "I was raised by my dad and he was usually away, so I didn't have the luxury of staying sick for long since I always had to figure myself out. Even malaria couldn't keep me down."

She felt warm hearing his voice, the casual way he talked about the difficult parts of his life like he was merely pointing out the unpredictable Houston weather.

"That's a relief then," Ibelema said with a curt nod. "I mean, Barb was worried."

"Sorry, I told them not to fuss. Tiwa's more important." Tonye tossed his used tissues and empty water bottles into the trashcan. "I don't think I'm contagious anymore. Wouldn't have invited you in if I was."

"Really?"

Caught in his own lie, he made a naughty child's face. "Okay, I definitely still would have."

She unzipped the cooler. "Thanks for your consideration."

"That smells good."

She almost jumped out of her skin at the closeness of his voice. He stood against her back as he peeked over her shoulder down at the cooler. His slightly overgrown beard did little to hide the sharpened edges of his face, which meant he probably hadn't eaten much the last few days. She suddenly was filled with remorse for not calling him, for not being there to take care of him when he needed her.

Ibelema smacked his arm. "Why didn't you call me?"

He looked surprised. "I...after the gala, I didn't—"

"You should have let me know you weren't feeling well."

"I know. I just thought—"

"It doesn't matter, Tonye."

He stepped back from her. "W—what doesn't matter?"

If she could get the awkwardness out of the way, maybe he would tell her what really happened. "I know something else went on that night. And Kay and Barb know what it is." She met his eyes. "I trust them, and they trust you."

He fiddled with his bottle on the counter. "Why would you think they trust me?"

She stifled a laugh. "Barb sent me here, and they clearly want something to happen between us. They wouldn't want that if you weren't a good person."

Tonye closed the gap between them in half a step. "And what about you? Do you trust me?"

She couldn't look away from his buttery smile. As dangerous as he seemed, she had never felt this safe with any man. During the months Kenneth tried to date her, she'd never felt free. With Tonye, it was clear that he didn't expect her to be anything other than herself, something she'd never experienced before. Even her own dad was always trying to change the things about her that he didn't like.

"Are you still in love with me?" she hesitated to ask.

"It's pretty obvious," he said, leaning toward her face.

His sweet breath was distracting—when did he find time to pop a mint? He'd really been expecting her to come?

"Okay, but do you like me?" Loving someone and liking them didn't always mean the same thing.

He seemed to understand what she meant. "A lot."

"What do you like about me?" There was never a shortage of men who liked her, but they rarely followed through. What Tonye liked wasn't as important as what he didn't like. Most guys never had a problem telling her what they didn't like about her, which often included how "intimidating" she could be.

"Scratch that," she said, standing up straighter. "What don't you like about me?"

His brow furrowed. "I'll have to think hard about that." He was dodging the question.

"Then...why do you like me?"

"I didn't think I needed a reason to like you."

"But there's something that made you like me."

"I guess." He appeared to rethink the question. "If I had to give a reason, it might be because you're the most amazing woman I've ever met."

"But you don't know that much about me."

"I know enough."

"How? I haven't dated much, so I'm not really good at these things."

"I know."

"I'm a virgin," she blurted out, just to see his reaction. Would-be suitors were always speechless when she revealed that fun fact. In her early teens, she'd made a deal with herself that when she first had sex it would be with her husband. But in college, the decision turned out to be much harder than she'd ever thought. It got easier with time, though. She always seemed to attract men who didn't know how to love her the right way, which made it hard for her to love them back.

"Okay," Tonye replied slowly, and watched her as if he didn't understand what she was saying. Suddenly, his face split into a gorgeous smile. "Why did you just tell me that?"

"Because if you're doing all this to sleep with me, I don't know if I'm any good at that either."

He looked shocked for a second, then laughed, shaking his

head. “That’s not how that works.”

“Then how? I don’t know how” —she waved her finger from her chest to his chest— “this works.”

Tonye grabbed her hand and placed it on his chest. “It will work, Ibelema. For the first time in my life, I have no doubt it’ll work.”

She could feel his thundering heart under her palm. “How? You’ll go back—”

His lips stopped her from speaking another word, and for a moment, she just stood there not sure what to do. His tongue expertly darted into her mouth, and he tugged on her lips with his. A jolt of something she’d never felt before pulsed through her veins, throwing her off balance, but Tonye held her steady, until he broke the kiss, and leaned back to gaze at her. She hoped he wouldn’t notice she was freaking out.

“I don’t want you to catch anything,” Tonye said, his voice low and husky.

Ibelema opened her mouth, but she didn’t actually hear what she said. Maybe she didn’t say anything. Even if he was still contagious, who cared?

His mouth twitched, amused. “Can I kiss you again?”

“Yes?” She couldn’t believe how ridiculous she sounded.

“You don’t know?”

“I already told you, I’m not good at this.”

“I call bull. I just took a test drive, and it was pretty good.”

Now he was pulling her legs. She tried and failed to wiggle out of his arms. Not one of the men she’d kissed in the past had given rave reviews. When Kenneth first kissed her, she’d forgotten to close her eyes, so every time after that, he’d looked at her like she was doing something wrong.

“You’re perfect, Ibelema Pepple.”

Her face felt hot. "Then you can—"

His mouth met hers again. This time, his kiss was more urgent, like he'd held back the last time. She couldn't pull away, didn't want to. His tongue sent piercing slivers of joy and something else through her, and she reached up to slip her arms around his neck. She had no idea how much time passed. All she could think about was the strange heat spreading from the back of her knees to her chest and landing in the most unsettling place.

When Tonye finally pulled away, Ibelema couldn't make eye contact with him. He had reached inside of her and drawn out these strange sensations she'd never expected to feel. She rested her head on his chest, wishing she could find some other way to tell him to keep kissing her.

"You didn't like it?" Tonye whispered in her ear.

She smiled shyly at his naughty grin. "I think we should try again."

His eyes widened, and she tried not to laugh as Tonye pulled her closer without hesitation. She leaned in when he tilted her head toward his, and made her mouth burn. His strong hands flowed over her like a light breeze, and she thought she heard herself gasp, but was too caught up in the moment to think about the embarrassing sounds she was making. Was this what it felt like to be kissed by a man who loved you? Who wanted you more than anyone else? Her lips were still on fire when he pulled away again.

"You owe me a dance," Tonye said.

Still dazed, Ibelema didn't realize he was waiting for her to respond. "Oh, like right now? There's no music, though."

"We don't need music." His thumb caressed her mouth. "I don't just like you, Ibelema. I love you. I'm in love with you."

She gazed into his gentle eyes, trying to find something, anything that would snap her out of this madness. But the warmth was spreading all over her again. Maybe this was what love felt like.

"Dance with me," Tonye said, taking her hand. "Just like you do in my dreams."

Ibelema pressed her body against him, and as they slow-danced around the kitchen in the heavenly silence, he said the words again and again, and she knew he meant them with his entire being.

Long after she finally tore herself away and drove home, her whole body still throbbed from his soft kisses, leaving her with no doubt.

She had finally met the man she wanted to kiss for the rest of her life.

19

The auditorium was packed with young people for the special service, but Silas was able to find an empty seat beside an older Black woman in the pew next to the side door underneath the exit sign. Worship was in full force, and his personal superstar graced the stage with her guitar. Ibelema looked incredible, the spotlight glowing on her as if the sun itself had followed her inside.

He couldn't tear his eyes away from her, this quirky woman who said things straight and behaved without pretense. Her face was like a song, every emotion easily read, and right now, he could tell she was about to cry. How could a woman so strong be so fragile? No, she wasn't fragile. She just wasn't afraid to show her weakness. She didn't hesitate to tell him that she knew nothing about men, and yet as the night wore on, she had stopped him here and there to give feedback about how she wanted to be kissed and held. Strength and weakness in one. Her strong will demanded his respect. Her softness made him want to protect her.

"My God in heaven," Silas whispered to himself. He was hopelessly in love.

Just months ago, he'd been content with his life. He never minded the solitude, and enjoyed the freedom to come and go without the burden of others' expectations. Whenever he'd met a woman who interested him, he might date her a while—if she knew what she was doing, a while might turn into a few months—but none of them ever captured his thoughts like Ibelema.

"He's calling you," his songbird sang again.

Church was the wrong place for these thoughts, but their passionate kisses came to his mind again. They had made out until almost midnight, and since he hadn't wanted her driving late, he'd begged her to leave, but she kept asking him to touch her again. When he finally walked her outside, he kissed her and told her that he loved her for the hundredth time. She had kissed his cheek with a soft smile, and she didn't need to say anything for him to know how she felt.

Silas took a deep breath, surrounded by the great cloud of witnesses. How was it so easy for him to tell the woman that he loved her? If he didn't know better, he'd think she cast some juju on him. Yet, he had no doubt that he did love her, and that he could love her for the rest of his life.

"There comes a time," Ibelema was speaking on stage. "When nothing makes sense, and still, you get the sense that everything is exactly as it should be, like everything is coming together in some crazy way." She paused, as if overwhelmed. "You have to open your heart and let go of your hurt so you can remember who you are. Because we could stand here and sing a hundred songs and still never get it. And 30, 50 years from now, you could have everything you imagined. But if you didn't have the most important thing in your life, what would be the point?"

Ibelema was crying on stage as she dropped to her knees. With her hands lifted high, she seemed so pure, and he wondered if maybe he'd tainted her by thinking she could love someone like him. He didn't deserve a woman like her, but it didn't matter. She'd already told him she was his. He just needed to remember who he was. No matter what, he couldn't go back to how he used to be. He had to move forward, go back home and fix his mess. Maybe then he would be more deserving of Ibelema's true love.

The crowd burst out in applause, but Silas didn't move. He couldn't raise his hands. A moment passed, and suddenly he didn't hear her voice anymore. The auditorium went quiet, and he felt a presence drape over him like a weighted blanket. He was warm all over, but he wasn't sweating. The woman beside him swayed from side to side seemingly in rapture until she bumped into him.

"Sorry," the woman said.

"No problem," he said.

She stared at him. "You're Silas Harry."

His heart did a sharp turn in his chest, but the more he looked at her smiling face, the more the knot in his chest loosened. He nodded, waiting for her reaction.

She inclined her head in a sort of bow. "It's going to be okay, Silas Harry."

He tried to speak, but could only nod again. The stranger looked as though she had more to say, but she just patted his arm before facing the stage, where the minister began to pray.

Silas snuck out of the auditorium and nearly bumped into a man in the hallway. "Sorry," he said, and started to walk away.

"Wait," the man called. "You're the main lead in IB's film, right?" His face twisted into one of those insincere smiles Christians use to disarm you. He was probably one of those self-righteous douchebags who thought he could do no wrong. "Thanks for looking out for my girl. I'm Kenneth."

Silas gripped the man's hand a little harder than necessary. He'd heard the name before but didn't think much about it. Clearly, there was something here. Was this the man who had broken her heart?

"Are you the guy?" Silas asked.

"The guy?"

"Who was supposed to marry her?"

Kenneth's eyes went cold as he yanked his hand from Silas' death grip.

Silas couldn't help himself. "Thanks for not marrying her," he said, walking away with a grin. When he looked back, the guy was gone. Kenneth, who did he think he was calling IB 'his' girl?

The whole movie team was meeting at the smaller chapel after the worship service. As Silas left the main building, Ibelema was walking toward the chapel.

"Hi, Sugar," Silas greeted her, laughing at her wide-eyed reaction. It was obvious that she wasn't sure how to behave after their make-out session. She was so cute that he wanted to grab her and take her somewhere they could be alone.

"Are you okay?" Her voice was hoarse.

"Yeah. Why?"

"You just seem different," she said, giving him a curious look.

Silas wanted to ask about Kenneth but decided against it. He almost took her hand as they walked to the other building. "You don't sound too good."

Ibelema eyed him. "Yeah, someone said he wasn't

contagious."

He touched her forehead and she didn't move away from his hand. They were at the front of the chapel, and behind them, people were streaming out of the main church building.

"Sorry," he said. "I think we had a little too much fun."

Her shy smile at his words was so pretty. "You look handsome in your suit." She patted his arm and strode ahead of him into the chapel. Almost everyone was there, dressed for one of the final scenes that took place in the church.

Silas found Daniel with Michael and two white men. The strangers looked like the profiles on their website. Daniel had told him about them, and Silas helped cover the expenses.

"I'm Ibelema—nice to meet you," she introduced herself, shaking hands with the two men.

"This is Austin," Michael said with a wide grin, pointing to the bearded guy, "and Elliot," the clean-shaven guy with big square glasses. "They're from Shoot Me Studios, and they make killer videos for all types of production."

Ibelema gasped and held a hand over her mouth. "You're kidding, right?"

"Nope," Austin said. "You probably didn't get our email. We heard about your project and would like to help you get ready for the TIFF."

"What we've seen of your film looks incredible," Elliot said. "We're pumped to help."

Ibelema cast a confused glance between Silas and Daniel before looking back at the men. "I can't afford you."

Silas laughed as Austin stroked his full salt-and-pepper beard. "You don't need to pay us anything," Austin said. "And you can check out our website so you know we're legit."

"I know you're legit." Ibelema accepted the tablet Michael

handed her. She moved closer to Silas, and his pulse fluttered, even though she probably gave it no thought and just wanted to share the moment with him. Ibelema scrolled through the featured shorts, a skateboard documentary, and a wedding film. Her mouth formed an O shape in amazement.

"We're filming the last scenes this week," Daniel said to the filmmaking duo. "What's the next step?"

Austin snapped his fingers. "That's why we're here. If you're game, we can help with these final scenes, then go through all the other scenes and make adjustments. Then if you agree with our initial edits, we can start editing the whole film."

"I'm game," Ibelema said a little too loudly.

"And you're doing this out of the goodness of your heart?" Efe jumped in. As usual, she had appeared out of nowhere, and Chanel tagged along.

"Not exactly," Elliot replied.

"Someone already paid you," Chanel said.

"It's probably the same person who bought the camera," Efe said.

Silas pretended not to notice when Ibelema glanced at him. He smiled at Daniel's poker face. If he hadn't been there when Daniel had worked out the details with him, he would have thought he imagined the whole discussion to help out with the edits.

"Can you tell me who paid you?" Ibelema asked.

"We're sworn to secrecy," Austin explained. "All I can say is someone paid for our services and sent a brief description of your work. But from what Michael here showed us, we're more excited to work with you, not just for this project, but for future films too."

"Future films?" Ibelema asked, with a nervous frown.

"This can't be your only film idea. You're a one-of-a-kind

storyteller—you have to keep making more."

Ibelema turned away from the studio heads. "I don't know what to say." Efe hugged her friend in response.

Silas watched her eyes shining with tears. Was Ibelema crying because she was happy, or had he overstepped? Maybe he should have asked Austin and Elliot to wait until Ibelema responded to their email. But then she might never have responded.

"This is so surreal. First the camera, that spam email turning out to be real, and..." She looked at Silas. "Too many things are going good all at once."

She was so happy she was freaking out. Silas caught himself before he grabbed her hand. Too late. He could feel the weight of their stares on him.

"Should we leave y'all alone?" Efe teased.

Ibelema smacked Efe's arm and faced Austin and Elliot. "I don't fully understand what's going on, but thank you."

"It's our pleasure," they said in unison. "Then are we ready to get to work?" Elliot asked.

Ibelema nodded, and everyone cheered, dispersing to different areas of the hall. Daniel took the two men to one of the offices, probably to look over more footage. Ibelema went to check on the set while Efe and Chanel pulled Silas aside.

"We know it was you," Chanel said, with a smirk.

"Definitely," Efe echoed. "Good going, big bro."

Silas tried to act unaffected, but he knew he wasn't fooling them. Efe and Chanel had a playful way of disarming him. Sometimes, it really felt like he'd gained two younger sisters. He reminded himself again that he had to try and keep in touch with them even after he left.

"Why would you think it was me?" Silas asked.

Efe was distracted. "IB's looking at us," she whispered, pulling Chanel away seconds before Ibelema walked toward him.

Ibelema scanned the hall, as if to make sure no one was paying close attention to them. "I know what you did," she said, her pretty eyes bright.

"What are you talking about?"

"I've noticed that a lot of good things have been happening to me since you showed up in my life." She threw him that same smoldering look she'd given him before she asked him to kiss her again and again. "Thank you, Datonye Banigo. I promise you won't regret falling in love with me."

Warmth spread inside his chest. He wanted to hold her, kiss her, and hear her whisper to him like she did that night. He didn't realize he'd reached for her until she smacked his hand away.

"Boy, not here. We got work to do."

She left him standing there with a silly smile on his face.

20

On Phoebe's wedding day, Ibelema got to church early to coordinate with Tari and the rest of the women so everything could be in order.

By 3 pm, the seats in the outdoor courtyard were almost full and people kept trickling in. The sun was bright and almost too hot, but the light breeze kept everyone happy.

Ibelema waited by the double glass doors in the chapel as the rest of the bridal party gathered to enter the courtyard. Hannah, the flower girl was talking awkwardly with Eli to the side, and he never looked happier.

Ibelema had been worried about Eli the most, but watching him now made her smile. Almost eight months after their parents' death, the Teka kids seemed like they were doing better, and the bride had plenty to do with their recovery. It was an odd but wonderful miracle that Abe managed to find someone like

Phoebe, someone with the same gentle, easygoing heart of gold that made Mama Teka so lovable.

"They're so cute," Efe cooed, beside Ibelema. She loved children and volunteered in the elementary ministry.

"Where were you?" Ibelema asked.

"Arguing with Kenneth about the—"

"Where's Kimani?" She didn't want anything to ruin her mood right now.

Efe seemed to catch on. "Trying to fix Thandi's hair. Houston humidity strikes again." Efe looked her up and down. "You look different somehow. Maybe it's the dress? Or..."

"We're wearing the same material," Ibelema cut in, ignoring Efe's twinkling smile.

"Everyone and their mama know something's going on between y'all. You better start talking before I ask him." Efe nudged her.

A group of guests dressed in African traditional attire approached the doors. Ibelema showed them to the empty seats at the back of the courtyard and returned to her post. She still hadn't told anyone about her deepening relationship with Tonye. They'd gone on more dates, and hung out with Barb and Kay, but she refused to go back to his house because she didn't think she would make it out unscathed again. Their make-out sessions were spiraling out of control, and Ibelema still couldn't wrap her head around how much she loved his touch. It was as if after years of playing dead, her body had come alive and there was no going back.

"Did you find Judah?" Efe asked.

Dressed in a simple collared shirt and black jeans, Daniel walked toward them carrying two duffel bags. "He's outside. After I drop this off, I'll go help him with parking and stuff."

Ibelema eyed him. "I thought you'd finally wear a suit."

"Is Tonye here yet?" he asked.

Daniel's intuition was as annoying as Kimani's. "Why do you think he's coming? Did you talk to him?"

Efe chuckled. "Again, who do you think you're fooling?"

A cold stare instantly replaced the amusement in Daniel's eyes. Ibelema turned and saw Eden walking toward them. Eden was staring at Daniel.

"Hi," Eden greeted, with an awkward wave meant more for Daniel than anyone else. Eden was one of the most confident women Ibelema knew, but whenever Daniel was concerned, Eden always seemed out of sorts. And Daniel was even worse. Kimani described Daniel's behavior toward Eden as "borderline rude." And Daniel was hardly rude to anyone.

He barely acknowledged Eden's bubbly greeting and stalked away as if someone had annoyed him.

Eden's violet eyes flashed with irritation. "Why is he always like that?"

Ibelema smothered her laugh. If even Chanel could see it, why were the two people involved so clueless? Kimani joked that Daniel probably didn't like that he had a thing for Eden, so he mostly ignored her, which only made Eden more interested in him because no one ignored Eden Kane. With her alabaster skin and white-blond hair, she stood out too much to be ignored.

Efe shook her head. "Wow, Chanel was right."

"Right about what?" Eden asked, starry-eyed. She was such a girl sometimes.

"Don't worry about it," Efe replied. "Daniel's a trip." She peered outside toward the courtyard. "We might need those extra chairs. It's getting full, and our Naija people just started showing up. The reception's going to be crazy."

Ibelema scanned the open space. Since the wedding was this packed, no one might notice Tonye. She'd never taken a plus-one to a wedding before, but she had invited him last minute because she thought they might have fun.

Near the doors, the rest of the bridal party was almost complete. Kimani and her preteen daughter Thandi showed up in their stunning blue gowns. Thandi hugged Ibelema, then Efe, but the biggest hug was reserved for her favorite, Eden.

"You look gorgeous," Ibelema said, smoothing flyaway curls behind Thandi's ears.

"Nothing hairspray and pins couldn't fix," Kimani said, looking her up and down. "You look nice. Where's Tonye?"

Ibelema opened her mouth to protest, and Efe cackled. "You guys are acting like I don't ever dress up."

"Who said?" Kimani adjusted the ruffle on Ibelema's shoulder. "Just haven't seen you show even a bare shoulder since our last trip to the beach."

Ibelema slapped away Kimani's hand. Aunty Osagie had sewn the dress for her, raving that it showed off her killer shape. For months she'd barely looked at the dress, but once Tonye agreed to come to the wedding, it suddenly seemed like the best option in her closet.

"Blame my mom and Aunty," Ibelema said.

"I knew I could trust Aunty Osagie," Efe crooned. "She knows how to make your shape show well-well," she added, drawing an S with her finger.

"Get a grip," Ibelema mumbled, dodging Efe's playful hands.

Kimani and Thandi laughed. "I like the dress too," Thandi chimed in.

Ibelema squeezed Thandi again. "And I love your dress."

"Thandi." A girl dressed in the same shade as Thandi's blue

shuffled toward them. "I found a cute hairband for you." She looked lovely and lean in her bridesmaid dress.

Phoebe had chosen her best friend Rue as her maid of honor, but Phoebe also wanted Darah and Thandi to round out her train with the two boys escorting them. Darah was walking in with Clement, while Thandi was paired with Marcus, Phoebe's soon-to-be adopted brother.

Darah's eyes grew big. "Ms. IB, wow. I almost didn't recognize you in that dress. Stunning—I love it." Instead of a low bun like Thandi's, Darah's hair flowed free and full around her face. She'd grown again since the last time Ibelema saw her months ago. How tall was she going to get?

Ibelema could feel Kimani's gaze. "Why is everyone acting like I don't dress up?"

"You're always pretty though," Darah said. "Even if you're wearing some quirky African jumpsuit or pants or mom jeans, or—"

"I get the point," Ibelema cut her off. Teasing or not, it was good to see that Darah's unapologetic way of speaking hadn't changed. She didn't miss the days she taught Sunday school for Darah and Thandi's class. The girl had too many questions about life and never accepted any simple responses. Darah Teka spoke and behaved like a grown woman trapped in a preteen's body.

"Are you excited?" Ibelema asked.

Darah's smile was blinding. "You have no idea. Being the only girl in the family got old quick. I can't wait for Phoebe to knock these knuckleheads into shape."

"I know you're not talking." A lanky teen dressed in a suit tugged on Darah's hair as he walked by. "You're worse than all of us put together."

"Watch the hair," Darah growled at her older brother,

Clement. "See? Knucklehead."

Clement waved. "How you doing, IB?"

Ibelema looked the much younger man up and down. "So, you're grown now?"

"That's Ms. IB to you, punk." Darah dodged his outstretched hand. "Come on, Thandi, let's put this on your hair. That okay, Aunty Mani?" The two girls hurried to the nearest restroom without hearing her response.

"They're gonna call us soon," Kimani cried after them.

"Where's Phoebe?" Ibelema asked. "Is she ready?"

Kimani snorted. "That girl been ready. She's about to explode."

"I hope I'm like that when my man comes," Efe said.

Eden sighed. "Me too."

"You still haven't answered," Kimani said, turning to Ibelema. "Where's your man?"

"IB has a man?" Eden asked, a pretty smile curving her lips.

Ibelema waved them off and handed a guest the program as the music from the courtyard changed into a soft melody. From the other building, the pastor readied to enter the courtyard alongside Abe Teka and his brother. The crowd cheered as Bart gestured with his hands to rile them up.

"He looks good," Efe let out a low whistle.

"Phoebe's gonna cry when she sees him," Kimani said.

"Abe too, but his brother is fine." Efe shook her head. "Too bad he doesn't like Black women."

"And you know that how?"

"I know many things you guys have no idea about," Efe replied, with no further explanation.

Ibelema chuckled at the nervous groom waiting at the entrance. For a moment the image was replaced by Tonye dressed in a tuxedo, and her stomach flipped over as if it was her own wedding. Her face warmed just thinking of his beautiful smile.

"Earth to IB," Kimani said, as Thandi and Darah appeared beside her.

Ibelema hugged her friend. "You look gorgeous, Kimani."

Kimani smiled. "You're not off the hook," she whispered, grabbing Thandi and Darah and shepherding them to the line. Thandi fell in beside Phoebe's handsome little brother, who was freakishly tall for his age. Phoebe said he played football.

"You look beautiful," Marcus said to Thandi, and she ducked her head with a blush.

"We need to watch that boy," Efe said.

Ibelema laughed and did a final check of the bridal party as Phoebe's maid of honor got into position. Everyone was lined up in the order they would enter. Ibelema checked the other end of the chapel, where Phoebe—looking radiant in her flowing white dress—approached the glass doors escorted by her dad.

The music changed again, and Eden signaled the train to get moving. One by one, they exited the chapel and entered the courtyard until only Phoebe and her dad were left.

Phoebe smiled at Ibelema and Eden. "Thank you so much, ladies."

As Phoebe walked down the flowered path toward the courtyard, Ibelema felt a tear sliding down her cheek. It was all too beautiful. Eden gave a peace sign and strolled outside.

Ibelema shut the double doors and stood there alone.

Someone tapped her shoulder. She turned to a kiss on her forehead.

"Hello, my love."

21

"You're here," she said, looking pleased to see him. She planted a quick kiss on his lips, not bothering to check if anyone was around. The chapel was empty as she hugged him tight.

"Aren't you watching the ceremony?" Silas asked.

"I would start crying if I saw Phoebe again. Like sobbing for real."

He laughed at her adorable admission. Strength and weakness, his Ibelema. "When do you think it'll be our turn?"

Her mouth dropped in surprise. "Are you serious?"

"As much as I love kissing you, I don't know how much longer I can wait to have the rest of you." He expected her to panic at his words, but she grinned at him as if she wanted the same thing.

He stroked her hair just as an older couple was walking from the courtyard, and Ibelema jerked and opened the chapel door for them. The woman looked like Ibelema, though shorter and lighter in complexion.

"You're leaving already?" Ibelema stepped away from Silas.

The man and the woman eyed Silas and her dad's stare turned into a glare.

Silas tilted his head in greeting. "*Dede, Í báāmá.*" Father, good morning.

Her dad eyed him with a mix of skepticism and curiosity.

"My name is Tonye, sir. It's really nice to meet you." Silas extended his hand.

Mr. Pepple shook his hand. "Tonye, *toro*?"

"*Ibim*, Sir." He turned to the woman gawking at him. "Good morning, Mommy. It's good to meet you too."

Her warm smile came easier than her husband's. "It's good to be met. You're Ibani?"

Silas nodded, grinning wide. "Born in Port Harcourt, but my dad is from Bonny."

Her parents exchanged smiles as their eyes drank him in. They were sizing him up.

Ibelema stepped in between Silas and her parents. "You'll be late."

Her dad tossed Silas an unreadable look, not appearing happy or angry.

Ibelema's mom flung her arms around her daughter. "You do well, my child," she said in a too-loud voice.

"Mom," Ibelema protested.

Silas would have laughed if her dad wasn't watching him. "Are you the boy from Nigeria who's playing the Reverend?" Mr. Pepple asked.

"Yes." Wait, her dad knew details about the film? Even Ibelema looked surprised. "Your daughter's very talented. We're all excited for this film, and we hope it's the start of something amazing for her, and for us."

"Us?" Her dad's stare pinned Ibelema.

"Dad, he meant—"

Silas knew what the man wanted to know. "If it's okay with you, I would like to come and talk to you about your daughter, sir." Silas held his gaze until the older man nodded.

"You can come. Ibelema will let you know." Mr. Pepple put his hand on his wife's shoulder and walked across the chapel.

Her mom's smile was reassuring as she followed after her husband. "We'll be seeing you soon."

The music was playing again outside the courtyard. A very pale woman showed up and smiled at Silas before pulling Ibelema away.

"I have to go," Ibelema said. "Will you be okay?"

"Of course," Silas replied. "I'll go in. We'll catch up later."

When Silas entered the courtyard, he found a space at the back. The courtyard overlooked a small lake, and the view was lovely. The bride and groom were doing some sort of ceremony with sand. Ibelema had told him their love story, and they looked exactly how he had pictured them.

After the ceremony ended, he followed the guests to the reception in the church gym. He was standing around admiring the beautiful decorations when Efe skipped over with a bright smile.

"Hey, big bro. Looking dapper."

"Same for you," he returned the compliment. "Like that style on you, sis."

Efe did a little turn and laughed. "IB will be busy for a bit. Wanna sit with the others until she comes to get you?" She pointed a finger toward a table on the side, where he recognized

Michael and others from Ibelema's production. Silas went to sit beside Chanel and Jackie, who were teasing Michael about his colorful bowtie and suspenders.

With plenty dancing, the bridal party entered the hall. A woman introduced the families and made everyone laugh. Then the couple danced their first dance.

Ibelema appeared near the DJ. The lights dimmed throughout the hall, and a screen projected on the front wall, the sounds of a soft instrumental wafting into the room.

An old home video of a woman dancing with her teenage son showed on the large screen. The son twirled his mom around him and her joyful laughter filled the hall. The video cut to another shot of the same woman dancing with her son, who looked older now, and then another scene of them dancing in a living room with people laughing around them.

"Wow," Jackie muttered. "It's Abe dancing with his mom through the years."

IB had mentioned that the groom's mother died last year, so this was a tribute to her. From the surprised look on the groom's face in the front, the tribute was probably his wife's idea. Silas could feel the love radiating between them.

He looked toward the DJ and heard Ibelema's voice, his songbird crooning softly. He didn't know the song, but it sounded beautiful, and he suddenly felt overwhelmed by the mood, so he closed his eyes. His own mother was alive, yet he was on bad terms with her. Maybe it was time to forget the past and move on.

As Ibelema's voice and the mother-son images on the screen faded, the lights came back on. The hall erupted in applause, many people wiping their faces. Mrs. Teka must have been loved by the church.

After the bride danced with her father, Silas went to look for his woman. It would have been nice to have a drink, but this was a church wedding, so that was a bust. He found a setup that looked like a bar, but it was a candy station.

"Hi, Silas. You know the couple?"

He nearly bumped into the table at hearing someone call his name. It was the woman who had recognized him during the youth service at church.

"I know the bride through my friend," he said, though it felt wrong to call Ibelema a friend.

The woman flashed a knowing smile. "Ibelema is a wonderful...friend. Amazing singer, too." She sighed. "What a wonderful wedding. So beautiful, right?"

Silas knew what she meant. The easy camaraderie between the guests seemed sincere, with laughter all around. Everyone looked thrilled to celebrate the couple, not a sad face in the crowd. Out of nowhere, a reggae beat made the crowd cheer, and people rushed to the dance floor.

"You made it." Daniel stopped by the station and pounded fists with Silas. "I see you met Ms. Jen. She's my aunt's best friend. Ms. Jen, this is Tonye."

"Small world," Silas said.

Ms. Jen's face changed as two guys walked over to the candy station, one of them being the best man.

"These look legit," the best man said, scanning the candy bar with a childlike grin.

Ms. Jen skirted around Silas and dashed off like someone was chasing her. Silas watched her go, wondering what she was about, but no one else seemed to notice.

The best man grabbed a handful of watermelon-shaped candies, and the younger guy with him reached for a chocolate bar. "You sound like an old man," the young one said. "That watermelon's got a chokehold on you."

"Mind yours," the best man brushed him off, extending a hand to Daniel and dapping him up.

Silas couldn't help staring at him. Something about the guy's face seemed familiar.

"Bart Teka," he said, introducing himself to Silas. "And this is Clement."

"Tonye Banigo," Silas said, shaking hands with them.

Someone called for Daniel, and he left Silas with the two guys. Silas noticed the younger one looking at him just like Silas was staring at Bart. Did Clement recognize him from one of his movies?

"Banigo?" Clement said. "You from Nigeria?"

Silas nodded. If he asked him that, he probably didn't recognize him. The boy looked at him as if he wanted to say something else, but a girl in a blue dress grabbed his arm. Clement seemed confused and looked back at Silas as he left with the girl.

Bart grabbed a handful of candy. "What part of Nigeria?"

"Lagos," he replied.

Bart looked disappointed. "One of my friends lives in Abuja."

"A woman?"

"Yeah, Geri. She left here last year."

Geri? What were the chances of her being the same person? At a New Year's party in Abuja, Hakeem—Silas' classmate from law school—had introduced him to an interesting Spanish-looking woman called Geri who said she lived in Houston.

"Geri, as in a Black Hispanic woman?"

Bart's eyes widened. "You know Geri?"

"I think so."

"Geraldine Peña?"

"Yeah, that was her name."

"How is she? Where did you see her?"

Silas grinned at the barrage of questions. "I met her through a friend. He said he was planning to propose soon."

Bart's mouth stayed open. "Propose? Like she's getting married?"

He had said too much. Was Geri this guy's ex-girlfriend? It did give that vibe. "That's all I know," Silas replied. He'd barely spoken to the woman because he didn't want to catch up with Hakeem, his filthy rich friend who was always up to no good.

Bart looked down at the candy like he wanted to toss it.

"You okay?" Silas asked.

Bart's head jerked as if he forgot Silas was standing there. "Yeah, I'm good," he replied, his voice tinged with sadness. "That's something. Geri's getting married. Makes sense."

For real, this guy seemed familiar. Maybe he'd run into him somewhere before. "Have you been to Nigeria?"

Bart shook his head. "Been to Ghana once, Senegal and Liberia too, but not Nigeria. Hasn't come on my radar till..." He trailed off.

The same girl in blue showed up again. "Bartimeus Teka, what are you still doing here? Everyone's looking for you."

"Doubt it," Bart shot back. The girl tugged on his arm and he popped another piece of candy into his mouth. "This is my sister, Darah. She thinks she's the wedding planner."

"That's because the wedding planner's tired of telling you where to be." The girl paused to smile at Silas. "Oh, I see...you're the reason Ms. IB's dressed up, aren't you? I saw her keep looking this way."

Silas couldn't help but smile. He looked around the hall and didn't see her.

"Don't mind this busybody," Bart said, leading her away. "See you around, Tony."

The siblings bickered as they walked away. Ibelema had said the Teka siblings were adopted at different ages, but no one would know watching them.

"I'm back," Ibelema's voice came from behind him.

He turned and his smile widened. She truly was the most beautiful woman alive. Ibelema took his hand and hugged him, but Silas stepped back just to drink her in again. He felt like the luckiest man to have her look at him like she was looking right now.

"Screw a drink." She was more intoxicating than any liquor in the world.

"What?" Ibelema chuckled. "I'm lost."

"Me too." He kissed the back of her hand. "I'm lost in you and loving it, my sugar. You're all I will ever need."

22

When Ibelema pulled into the driveway beside Tonye's car, she sat in the car for a minute. Since she lived with her parents, it had become inconvenient to always have to meet outdoors at a restaurant or the park, so she'd finally agreed to see him at home again.

Humming a tune, she grabbed the bag of fruits and the takeout Vietnamese food and walked up the gravel path to the door. In the daytime, the neighborhood was as quiet as that first night. The last time she was here, she'd almost lost all control, and she knew she was asking for trouble coming here again, but they hadn't spent much time alone since the wedding last weekend.

"Dang, you can sing."

The voice made Ibelema stop. She hadn't realized she was singing.

A middle-aged woman strolled across the field from the

neighbor's house wearing a straw hat, oversized sunglasses, and a silky two-piece casual set.

"And you're pretty too," the woman said, sizing her up. "I seen you come here before, so I just came to say hello. Are you Mr. Handsome's girl?"

Ibelema managed a smile. Mr. Handsome was an accurate nickname. "Yeah, I am." It felt good saying it aloud.

The woman's smile dimmed a little, and she glanced at the takeout bag in Ibelema's hand. "Well, you're lucky. He doesn't get many visitors. I only ever see him when he jogs some mornings."

The door opened behind them, and Tonye rushed out to take the bags from Ibelema. "Didn't know you would get here so fast," he said, sounding breathless.

Ibelema raised a brow. She told him she'd be here late afternoon, so why did he look surprised?

"Lordy," the woman swooned. "He looks even better without his glasses. Didn't see you running today, so was just saying hey to your girl."

Ibelema chuckled at Tonye's rapid blinking. At least he had the decency to look uncomfortable. He grabbed her hand and pulled her closer to him, clearly not sure what to do with this woman's unabashed fascination with him.

"The food's getting cold." He cleared his throat.

"Well, I'm not," the woman said in a suggestive voice. "If y'all need a little extra hot sauce for what y'all got going on, just let me know."

Now it was Ibelema's turn to be speechless. Tonye pulled her into the house with a "Thanks, have a good night," and shut the door as the woman bid them adieu.

Tonye dropped the takeout on the counter, pushed her against the wall and kissed her senseless. After a moment, Ibelema broke away from him and padded to the kitchen. She just got here and they were already losing it.

"I brought takeout and fruit," she said, trying to pivot the conversation or lack thereof.

Tonye slipped his arms around her waist and pressed butterfly kisses all over her neck. She bit her lips to keep from moaning. God, what was this man doing to her?

"You're so beautiful," he whispered.

His breath against her skin sent heat rushing up her back. She nudged him and he released her. Determined to distract him, she started unpacking the takeout.

"So, why's your middle-aged neighbor practically drooling over you?" Ibelema asked. "Do you go running shirtless or something?" Tonye made a face, and she shook her head. "Seriously?"

"It's hot out," he replied, with an innocent shrug.

"Right. I'm dating a thirst trap." After all, his alter ego, Silas Harry had pictures of him practically bursting out of tight shirts on the internet. This Tonye was wearing a fitted t-shirt over loose jeans, comfortable and without any flair. Still, his easy smile and sexy laugh made her pulse trip.

"I have no interest in seducing anyone whose initials aren't I.P."

Yeah, coming here again was a bad idea. He was having too much fun with this. She squinted at him. "Trying to seduce me, sir?"

He waved her off. "Just pulling your leg. You know that's not what I mean." He circled the counter and reached for her hand. A kiss here, a kiss there.

She eyed him. "Then what are you doing?"

Stepping closer, his deep brown eyes fixed on her with

intensity. "If anyone's doing the seducing, it's you. I'm the one going crazy here."

Ibelema drew in her lips and Tonye's gaze dipped to her mouth.

"Even as you vex for me, you're breathtaking. I missed you, my sugar in Sugar Land."

Her lips twitched as she fought a laugh. He was so corny it was good.

"My sweet puff-puff queen." His fingers poked her cheek. "My favorite kind of dessert."

The laughter bubbled out as he kissed her nose. "Are you toasting me right now?"

"Is it working?"

She placed her hands around his shoulders. "Keep going."

He pulled her against him. "It's only you I see, Ibelema. You in my arms is paradise. If I die now, I'll die a blessed man."

Ibelema smacked his shoulder. "God forbid. Don't say that."

His lips hovered over her mouth, and she forgot everything else. His touch made her yield to him, and she wondered why it was so easy to give herself to this man. Drawing her toward the couch and pulling her onto his lap, he continued to melt her willpower with devastating kisses. She'd never been kissed this way before; held like a jewel he was careful not to break. How did he manage to make her feel desired and loved at the same time? She wanted more, and more.

Ibelema pulled away to catch her breath, and leaned her head against his shoulder. "I love you."

"I love you too, Ibelema."

She smiled at the eagerness on his face. His fingers stroked her arms, sending thrills down her sides. "Ready to meet my parents?"

Tonye searched her face. "Your dad set a date?"

"Sunday," she said, planting a big kiss on his cheek.

He nodded as if imprinting the date on his mind. "In two days. That's perfect."

She snuggled against him and they sat in silence, Tonye's heart beating against her cheek. She could sit here forever if they had nothing else to do. A movie score she heard the other day started playing in her head, and she hummed the tune.

"You sound like heaven came down with you," he said.

"Oh boy. This your toasting is getting serious."

"I'm serious. When I wake up and when I go to sleep, I hear your voice, your songs. I keep thinking I could get used to listening to you for the rest of my life."

He grabbed her chin, but she turned away because she couldn't bear to look at him. With his open praise and unabashed declaration of wanting her, Ibelema wondered how he could actually feel that way.

"Look at me," he said, so she did. "I want you as my best friend, my playmate, my lover, my everything."

Her eyes watered and blurred her vision. "I want you too, Tonye." He hadn't said he wanted to marry her, but everything pointed to that. He was probably going to ask her dad when they talked on Sunday. Falling in love this fast was wild, yet it made perfect sense that she should marry him. There was just one thing.

Tonye's smile turned sad, just like when he'd talked about his mother on their Austin trip. "There's something I need to tell you."

She sat up in his arms. "Sure. Is it about your mom?"

"My mom? What about her?" He seemed annoyed. "I told my dad about you and he can't wait to meet you. He's been hoping for me to find the woman to make an honest man out of me."

"And that's me?" She smiled, imagining Tonye's dad. Would he like her?

"Definitely, sugar."

He kissed her, but she drew back before the kiss deepened. "And what about your mom?"

"What about her?"

She ignored the edge in his voice. "I want to meet her."

"Why? What does she have to do with this?"

"Everything."

"That lady's not part of my life."

"But she's a part of you. You can't just ignore that." She traced the outline of his mouth. "She's right here in Houston. I want to meet her, Tonye."

Tonye's hands dropped from her waist, taking his warmth with him. His eyes looked past her at the TV. She wasn't going to back down. If he wanted to get distant, she would stretch it a little. She got up and strolled to the kitchen.

He was at her side within seconds. "Please, don't leave."

"I'm not leaving. I brought dinner for us, remember?"

He watched her. "You're not upset?"

"I dropped a bomb on you, so how could I get mad?" She touched his cheek. "But I'm serious, Tonye. If we're doing this, whatever this is–"

He placed her hand against his beating heart. "You know what this is. I want you forever. I want to marry you."

Her legs weakened at the certainty in his voice, but she strengthened her resolve. "I want to marry you too. But first, I need to meet your mom."

Tonye frowned. "I don't want to see her, Ibelema."

"You came all the way to Houston for a reason." She tugged her hand free and pulled out the bag of tangerines. Who knew she'd have to use one now? "Remember that sermon from the conference with that one analogy about the rotten tangerine in the bag?"

"Baby, you can't ask me if I remember anything other than us kissing the night before that."

Her cheeks burned at their intense moment that night in his car. She had been finding it hard to concentrate after Tonye had awakened a part of her she didn't think existed. These days, even her quiet time was invaded by thoughts of him.

"Please, jog my memory," Tonye said.

She needed to marry this man before she did something she would regret. "Anyway. A bag of tangerines is like our heart, and each tangerine is a memory or feeling, like love, excitement or bitterness. So when one tangerine is bad, it's usually hidden until it goes bad, and the rot spreads everywhere."

He scowled at the bag of tangerines she'd carefully selected at the store.

Ibelema held out a tangerine to him. "You have every right to resent her for what she did. Her leaving like that, and forcing you and your dad to figure out your lives was terrible."

"Are you asking me to forgive her? Because I have. We can just ignore her and move on with our lives."

Ibelema shook her head. "I can't do that, Tonye. And neither can you. I want to meet your mom." She paused, wondering if what she wanted to say next would be going too far, but telling him was probably her best chance to make him relent. "I want our children to have a relationship with their grandmother."

Tonye's eyes went wide, then his face softened with a warm, childlike smile.

"Whether you want to admit it or not," she went on. "You know it's not a coincidence that you ended up here."

"It's not a coincidence. I came here to meet the love of my life. You." Tonye took the tangerine and pulled her closer. "But I can see how important this is to you."

Her heart fluttered. "I know this is hard for you, but before you meet my parents, I want to meet your mom."

"Before?"

"Yes. Knowing you, you're probably going to meet my dad and ask him a question, right?"

He grinned. "You know me."

"Then I want to be able to freely respond to you the way you want."

Tonye searched her face and sighed. "Okay. Let's go today."

"Today?" He was so impulsive. "I was thinking maybe tomorrow? You know, Saturday."

He grabbed his phone. "This can't wait."

Her pulse was in her mouth. "You sure?" One minute, the guy didn't want to see his mom, and now he was rushing her.

"Let's get it over with. I want you confident by the time I talk with your dad about our future." He raised his brows. "Is that good?"

Ibelema nodded with tears in her eyes, and this time, she was the one who pulled him closer for a kiss.

23

Silas looked over at Ibelema beaming at him in his passenger seat. Instead of enjoying her company at home, they were headed on some foolish mission to meet his mother.

Ibelema bounced in her seat as if they were going on a fun adventure. "Pearland is 5-10 miles from miles from here," she said. "Should I pull up the address on my phone?"

"Just distract me so I don't change my mind." A few days after talking with his dad, That Lady had texted him an address. Dad probably told her he was in Houston. He'd started to draft a text to let her know that he was driving to her house, but figured she didn't need to know. If she was home, then God really did want her to meet Ibelema.

"Should I sing you a song or something?" She was clearly pleased with herself.

"You're going to need more than a song to make this up to

me."

"What do you want?" She gave him a cheeky smile. "Actually, I know what you want, baby. That's why we're doing this, so we can fulfill all righteousness and get everything out of the way."

His head felt light. "Call me that again."

"Call you what?"

"Baby," he said, trying to mimic her voice.

She shrieked and covered her face. She probably hadn't noticed how the pet name had come out so easily. Adorable.

"What if this goes horribly wrong?" Tonye asked, mostly for himself.

"What if it goes very well?"

"I don't see a scenario where that's possible." He had ignored his mother for so long he didn't remember much about her. All he knew was that she'd remarried, but did she have kids? What did she do for a living? Had she reached the top of that corporate ladder she'd left him to chase after?

Why should he care if she was happy with her life or not anyway? A secret part of him wished she was miserable and regretted her choice every single day.

Ibelema placed her hand over his on the console. "You have every right to resent her for what she did. But don't you think your relationship with her has affected all your relationships, especially with women?"

The question triggered a mental montage of his failed dating history and trail of heartbroken women. Was that why he could never bring himself to commit to any of them? Thankfully, he didn't have that problem with Ibelema.

She squinted at him from the passenger seat. "You're probably thinking our relationship is different. But what if one day you start to see me the same way you see other women? What are you going to do then?"

"There's no what if because it will never happen."

"How can you be so sure?" Ibelema pressed, "There's still so much resentment and bitterness toward your mom, and that's why you don't trust women. If you can't forgive her, how do you know you'll forgive me when I hurt you too? Because I will hurt you. That's just how love's about."

He groaned. "You're not being fair."

"I know." She smiled, leaning back in her seat. "I'm yours either way. But before we go fully into what forever looks like, you need to work through your past with your mom."

Tonye gripped the steering wheel so tight his knuckles cracked. "I don't know about other women, but I trust you." No other woman knew about his mother.

Ibelema touched his cheek. "Then can you trust me with this? Please?"

How could he stay irritated when she was so precious? Yet another sign he was meant to spend the rest of his life with her. If reconciling with his mom made Ibelema happy and ready to be with him forever, then that was what he needed to do.

"We're in Pearland," she said, after a few moments of silence. "I know this area. It's a gated community." She pointed to the next street. "The entrance is coming up on the left."

The GPS echoed the command and Silas turned into the neighborhood. "You know someone here?" Silas asked, as they came to the gate.

"You do too," Ibelema said. "Wait, she's texted me the gate code before." She checked her phone, and he handed her his phone to confirm. She read the address aloud and frowned. "That's weird. Is your mom one of their neighbors?"

His stomach did a backflip. What if his mom was someone

Ibelema already knew? That would only make things harder. He saw her mouth open as the GPS announced that they had arrived at their destination, and the car pulled up in front of a two-story brick and stucco home. The fancy numbers on top of the garage matched the address in her text. Two cars were parked in the driveway.

"Tonye, what did you say your mom's name was?"

"Mfon, but I think she goes by something else now."

"There has to be an explanation for this." Ibelema opened the door and marched across the driveway.

Silas got out and grabbed her hand just as she rushed up the paved path. "What's going on?"

She looked spooked. "Let's just see first."

"Who lives here?" he asked, his heart pounding.

"IB? Tonye? What are you guys doing here?"

He turned to see Efe walking toward them. "You live here?"

"Yeah," Efe said, folding her arms across her chest. "What's going on, IB? I didn't know you were coming."

"Efe, is your mom expecting someone?" Ibelema walked ahead of Silas.

"Not that I know of," Efe replied.

"I didn't tell her we were coming," Silas said.

"Efe, is your mom inside?" Ibelema's voice sounded shaky. "I think we need to see her."

"No way." As Silas stared at Efe, the truth slapped him in his face so hard he stepped back. That was why she felt familiar.

"Are you okay?" Efe asked, her hand reaching out to him. "Why are you looking at me like that?"

Silas felt like throwing up. How could he have missed it? Efe looked exactly like the woman from the pictures Dad kept of his mother, the young and stunning beauty.

"Well, you're here, so let's go inside," Efe said, leading the way to the front door. "Mom is on a call, I think."

Silas didn't know how he moved. Ibelema grabbed his hand, giving him strength.

"We don't have to do this right now," Ibelema said.

"This can't wait." He gestured for her to go before him, but she didn't let go of his hand. Efe was waiting for them at the threshold, and her confused eyes dipped to their joined hands.

When they stepped inside the house, Efe left to go get her mom. Silas' eyes scanned the walls, studying Efe's family pictures, her dad, her little sister, her freaking mom. How could she do this to him? She had a whole separate family he'd never heard about, never even knew existed. All this time, he'd been hanging out with his...he couldn't even breathe the word.

He looked up as Efe appeared in the living room, and he turned away from her to see a framed photo of Efe's mom in a wedding gown with a man he assumed was Efe's father grinning beside her. Silas clenched his fists.

"Aunty Mercy," Ibelema called.

With a violent jerk, Silas came face-to-face with the trembling woman, Efe's mom, that lady who abandoned him and built a wonderful life for herself while her son was left reeling in Nigeria with a clueless father who couldn't move on because he never stopped loving her.

"T—t..." She couldn't even speak his name, guilt marring her face. She held a hand over her mouth. "How did you...?"

"Forgot you sent your address?" Silas felt Ibelema tap his arm.

"Relax," Ibelema whispered, looking anxious.

Silas realized he was squeezing his fists while still holding one of her hands. "Sorry," he murmured, relaxing his grip. He had to snap out of it and do what he came there to do. Smile, he reminded himself. He tried. He couldn't. He didn't know what look was on his face right now, but it must have been something. Even Efe looked scared.

"Hey...little sis." They were the only words that made sense to him. Efe was his little sister. He had two younger sisters.

"God." Efe's mom started sobbing and dropped on her knees. "I'm so sorry, Tonye."

Efe knelt beside her. "Mommy, what's going on? How do you know Tonye?"

"Efe," Ibelema said, "Maybe we should–"

"No, stay." Silas held onto her hand. He couldn't do this without her.

"Yes," Efe's mom croaked. "Please, stay." She seemed terrified of him. She gestured to the leather couch. "Please, have a seat first."

"No, we're not staying long. I only came because of the woman I want to marry."

Efe's mom blinked. "IB? You want to marry IB?"

"Already?" Efe cried.

Silas managed to smile. "Yeah, sis."

Efe's mom looked like a wounded stray as she hesitated to move closer to him. "That's great news, Tonye." She fidgeted with her hands and folded them behind her back. "I still can't believe you're here. I've thought about this day for so–"

"Please save it," he interrupted her, barely able to control the anger in his voice. "I didn't come here to play catch up with you." He turned to Ibelema. "You've met her. Can we go now?"

"What the heck is going on here?" Efe snapped. "How dare you talk to my mom like that?"

"Efe," Ibelema spoke up.

Her mom held up a hand and faced Efe. "He has every right to talk to me that way. He's–"

"I don't care who he is." Efe glared at him. "Who comes to someone's house uninvited and talks like this? Is my mom your mate? I can't believe I thought you were cool. You suck."

"Listen," Efe's mom shouted. "You can't talk to him like that either. He's your..." She inhaled a loud, shaky breath. "He's your older brother."

Efe's head reared back as if she'd been slapped. "What the–?"

"He's my son," their mother said again.

Silas felt Ibelema squeeze his hand again. As he watched a look of horror settle onto Efe's face, he wondered what was worse, her hearing about a brother she never knew existed, or him finding out that the woman had abandoned him to have other children who didn't know a lick about him. How could their mother be so messed up?

"I was married before I met your father," she said to Efe. "He's the child I had back in Nigeria." Her watery eyes turned to him. "Silas."

"My name is Tonye," he said, so loudly he felt Ibelema jump beside him. "You don't get to call me that."

"I'm sorry," their mother's voice broke.

Clearly stunned, Efe's gaze went between her mother and her newfound brother.

"I just have one question," Silas said. The same one he'd asked countless nights as a child. "Why did you leave like that? And how could you stay away so long? Did you even care about me at all?"

"I made a mistake," she whispered, as if afraid to speak the words.

Silas cursed. That was the worst possible answer she could

give. "What mistake did you make? Leaving me or having me?"

"Sil–Tonye, that's not what I meant. Please, if you could just let me explain."

"Explain what?" His heart was racing so fast he felt dizzy. "That I was just a hiccup in your big plans for your life?"

"No, that's not true. I–I just, I didn't, I–"

"You didn't care."

"No, I loved you, I've always loved you, I just wasn't ready to be your mother. I was afraid, and my parents–"

"Of course, blame it on your parents. They never wanted you to marry Dad, so they shipped you off to America." On one of the rare nights his dad drank too much, Silas had heard him rambling about how much her parents had disapproved of him as her choice.

"No, everything is my fault. And I truly regret all the harm I caused you. I'm so sorry, my son. I don't expect you to ever forgive me, but I–"

"I didn't come here for an apology," Silas said, through his teeth. "It's too late for that."

"No, it's not." Ibelema looked at him with soft eyes. "It's not too late, my love."

His legs buckled, and she held on to his waist. Hearing her call him that swept the anger out of him, and he remembered why he came here. He'd let her see him at his worst, but she was still looking at him like she always did, with love.

"I'm sorry," he said to Ibelema, then turned to Efe's mom—no, his mother. Ibelema wasn't going to let this go. He needed to have some sort of relationship with this woman, no matter how dysfunctional it might be. He was going to marry Ibelema and they would have children, and those children would ask about their grandmother.

"I'm sorry," Silas forced the words out to his mother. "I've been very rude to you." He bowed his head and turned to Efe. "Sorry for showing up like this. I think you're cool, too. I'm lucky to have a sister like you."

Efe had tears in her eyes. "I'm sorry, too."

"Si-Tonye..."

"I promise we'll talk again, soon...mom."

She burst into tears again. Silas knew he needed to call her that to show her and Ibelema that he had forgiven her and would do more going forward. Before she could say anything else, Silas marched out of the house holding on to Ibelema. He didn't stop or look at Ibelema until they got to the car.

"Please let me drive," she whispered.

He handed her the keys, slipped into the passenger seat, and closed his eyes. She didn't say a word to him on the drive back. Not that he could have responded to anything she said. His heart was so full he felt he might fall apart if he opened his mouth.

When they finally parked in front of his house, Ibelema placed her hand on his shoulder. "I'm so sorry."

"For what? I'm not mad at you." It wasn't her fault. She was right to make him go see his mom.

"But maybe the whole bag is already rotten," he added in a whisper.

"That's not true." Ibelema kissed his cheek. "I'm so proud of you. Proud to call you mine."

This beautiful songstress and her words. He was too tired to smile. "You're so going to make this up to me."

She flashed her gorgeous smile. "I will. You can have anything you want from me, my love."

He felt better just looking at her, like a weight was lifted off him, but at the same time, a new, heavier weight had been placed on his shoulders without him knowing. They still had more to talk about.

"You promise?" He would tell her tomorrow. Enough drama for one day.

"I promise, Tonye. I love you."

He could never get tired of hearing those words from her. "Say it again."

Her cheeks puffed up. "I love you, Tonye Banigo."

24

When Ibelema got home, her dad and mom were in the living room watching the news. “I cooked your favorite banga soup if you want some,” Mom said, eyes still on the TV.

Ibelema thanked her and made to go upstairs.

“I talked to my cousin back home,” Dad informed her. “He knows Tonye’s dad.”

Ibelema froze by the couch. At once, the tears she’d been holding in since leaving Tonye started flowing down her cheeks.

“What’s wrong?” Mom asked, rushing over.

Mom started crying too, and Ibelema found herself sandwiched between her parents on the couch. It had been a while since they’d sat together like this. A soft hand stroked her hair while Ibelema rested her head on Mom’s chest, and Dad’s heavy hand patted her back. As much as they gave her grief, they were still the best parents.

"Does this have anything to do with Tonye?" Mom asked.

Ibelema nodded, wondering how much to tell them. "His mom is here in Houston." Since Mom knew Efe's mom, it was only a matter of days before Mom would hear what happened.

"Then that should make things easier, right?" Mom smiled at Ibelema.

"His dad and mom aren't together," she explained.

Her parents were quiet for a while. "Does he have any siblings?" Mom asked.

"Yes..."

She was still reeling from the revelation. Tonye was Efe's half-brother—what a way for them to find out. She shouldn't have pushed him.

Standing outside Efe's house, Ibelema had known the exact moment Tonye realized the truth. She saw it play out on his face and in his body language, the way he'd stumbled backwards and clenched his fists like he wanted to punch someone. It was like she was watching someone else, not her Tonye. He hadn't said a word on the drive back. His sad face was turned to his window, but she saw from his reflection that he wasn't crying, just drained. After what his mom did to him, Tonye had every right not to talk to her, but Ibelema had forced him to confront her when neither of them was ready to face the other. And poor Efe. Once she got upstairs, she would text her to make sure Efe was alright. What a mess.

"Whatever God wants to be will be," Dad said, with a solemn nod, his hand still circling her back.

The doorbell rang, causing the three of them to look at one another in confusion. Who would show up this late to their house? Ibelema squeezed out of her parents' embrace and hurried to the door, half expecting to see Tonye. Dad was right behind her.

"Efe?"

"Good evening, Sir." Efe strolled into the house with a duffle bag slung over her shoulder like she'd been invited to a sleepover. "Can I stay here tonight? I can't deal with my parents right now."

Ibelema glanced sideways at her dad. "You can sleep here," he said. "But does your mom know you're here?"

Efe shook her head, and Mom hugged her. "Just come in," she said, leading Efe to the living room. "Have you eaten?"

"No, I just had to leave." Efe turned to Ibelema. "Did you tell them what happened?"

"I wasn't sure if I should."

Efe sighed and faced the parents. "I just found out I have a brother. My mom had a kid before marrying my dad–" she threw up her hands at Ibelema– "And he was coming at me like I have no right to be angry with her for not telling me."

"Impossible," Mom whispered. "Are you sure we're talking about the same Mercy?"

"And how did you find out?" Dad asked.

Efe fixed her eyes on Ibelema, as if for moral support, and she put her arms around Efe.

"I went over there with Tonye," Ibelema said. "I wanted to meet his mom, and..."

"Jesus Christ," Mom cried. "It's Tonye?"

Ibelema tried to explain as much as she could, and the conversation went on for so long that she didn't get a chance to talk one-on-one with Efe until after midnight. When they tried to go to sleep, Efe couldn't stop crying.

"I'm too angry to sleep," Efe admitted. "My mom is ridiculous. She couldn't even give me a good reason why she'd do something like that. How could she not tell me I had a brother?"

In a moment like this, Ibelema didn't know how to support

her friend. The whole scenario was still fresh. Efe's sweet mother was the same woman who abandoned Tonye.

"I just feel so bad for Tonye," Efe continued. "To hear his own mother call him a mistake...I can't imagine how he feels right now. My mom's the worst."

Ibelema rubbed her chest. It was hard to breathe. "She didn't really mean that he was a mistake."

"I know," Efe spat out. "But his face, IB. I mean, I can't believe I have a big brother. Tonye's my freaking brother."

"Yeah, it's crazy." She realized Efe was staring at her.

"And you're in love with him."

Ibelema sniffed back tears. "I am."

"Did he ask you to marry him? I don't see a ring."

She chuckled. "He will."

"And he told you everything?"

"Told me what?" Ibelema asked. Efe stayed silent, so she turned on her side to see Efe's face.

"How much he loves you." Laughing, Efe sunk into her pillow. "This is awesome. I always felt like you were my older sister, and now you actually are." She exhaled forcefully. "Aren't you mad at my mom, though?"

Ibelema turned her gaze toward the ceiling. Efe was acting odd, but considering everything that happened, maybe she was just overwhelmed.

"I'm mad at myself," Ibelema confessed. "I forced him to go to your place when he and Aunty Mercy weren't ready to meet. I mean, it's been so long since they last saw each other."

Efe let out a long sigh. "It's not your fault. It was going to come out anyway. I don't know who I'm more pissed off at, Mom or Dad. Apparently, Dad knew Mom when she was married to Tonye's dad. The whole thing is nuts. Did Tonye cry when you left our house?"

"No." He was probably waiting to be alone.

"That's even worse. You have to call him or go see him first thing tomorrow."

Ibelema swiped at her tears. "I'll text him. If there's anything I've learned about men, it's that sometimes you just need to give them space."

Still, she couldn't stop thinking about calling Tonye. She barely got any sleep, but she managed to hold out until dawn before texting him. He replied that he was okay and would call her later.

The next day, Efe finally went home in the afternoon, and Ibelema waited all Saturday for Tonye to call. He didn't. He only texted her good night and promised he would call tomorrow. As she wondered if he was still coming to see her dad, her sleep was just as restless as the night before.

The next day, she went to church and sang at all three services. Pastor Luke wanted to meet with them, and before she went into the meeting, Tonye finally called her.

"Hey, baby," Ibelema answered on the first ring. She wanted him to know exactly how she felt. "I missed you."

"Wow," he said, laughing. "I should disappear more often."

"Don't you dare. I'm just being nice to you right now."

"Thank you for that," Tonye said. "We're still on for me coming over, right?"

She felt her whole body relax. "Yeah, I thought you were rethinking–"

"Never. I've never been more certain in my life." His voice sounded hoarse. "But there's something we need to talk about before I come over."

Ibelema leaned against the wall of the office, where one of

the pastors gestured to her that she needed to come in. "Can we talk later? I'm still at church."

"Okay, call me as soon as you're free."

Now she was curious. "What's so important? Is this about Friday?"

"No...it's about something that happened back home."

More stuff about his past? "Tonye, I–"

"There's a scandal I was involved in. I didn't do anything wrong but–"

"Then there's nothing to talk about. You didn't do it, I trust you."

"It's not that simple—"

"It is for me, Tonye," she cut him off. "I only have one question."

"What is it?"

"Do you love me?"

He didn't hesitate. "More than anything or anyone."

She exhaled in relief. "And I love you, so it is that simple." Someone called her name from the office. "I have to go. I'll call you back."

When she got out of the meeting, Ibelema called him, but he didn't pick up. He was supposed to come over at 5, and he texted that he was on his way.

At home, her mom was so excited and kept checking the bay window overlooking the driveway from the dining room.

"He's here," Mom announced with infectious cheer.

Ibelema jogged outside. Tonye's car was parked in the driveway, and when he stepped out, dressed in an olive kaftan shirt with navy blue pants, he looked so handsome her heart leaped in her chest.

"Hello, love."

His words landed like a tender kiss. "It's so good to see you."

Tonye offered his arm, and they walked inside the house together. "Let's make this happen." He smiled, but it didn't quite reach his eyes.

"Don't be nervous. My parents are cool with you." After all, he was the first guy she'd ever brought home to meet them.

Once inside, Mom gave Tonye a big hug. "Welcome, my son." Mom squeezed him tightly, as if to tell him she knew everything. "We're having onunu and goat pepper soup if you want to stay for dinner."

"I love onunu," he said, his easy smile lighting up his face. "I haven't had it since I was a boy."

"Then you'll eat well today, my son." Mom's eyes twinkled as she touched his hand. "Your dad is in the study."

Ibelema led Tonye down the hallway. "I'll make onunu for you in the future," she promised.

He smiled like a kid. "That would be nice."

The study door was open. Dad was seated in an armchair reading his Bible. "Welcome, Tonye."

"Good evening, Sir." Tonye's voice was faint. He was clearly nervous.

Dad pointed to the chair beside him, and Tonye sat down. Ibelema brushed Tonye's shoulder as she left. Mom was waiting for her in the living room, grinning from ear to ear.

"What's the smile for?"

Mom did a little dance. "That looks like a man who's come here to ask for your hand."

An uncharacteristic giggle escaped Ibelema's lips. "Maybe."

Mom swatted Ibelema's behind playfully. "And you didn't think to warn me? He's so handsome."

"Yeah, he's perfect."

Hands joined, the two of them sat down together on the couch. "My beautiful girl, I've been praying so much for you and I just knew this would happen. Everything always works out for our good, if only we're patient." Her eyes were wet with happy tears. "Thank you for honoring me. You've been better than the daughter I asked God for."

Ibelema's eyes were blurry with unshed tears. "Thanks, Mommy."

"The way he looks at you, my princess. He clearly loves you." She wiped the tears from Ibelema's cheeks. "I can't believe it's finally happening."

She laughed when Mom flung her arms around her. "Slow down, Mommy. We don't know what he's saying, or what Dad will say."

Mom huffed. "Don't mind your dad, that softie. Sure, he'll throw his weight around, but he'll eventually give Tonye what he wants. Your dad loves you. He always tells me to be more patient with you."

That set off more tears. "Dad says that?"

"Don't you know your dad's your biggest fan?" She got up suddenly to grab her purse from the kitchen before returning to the sofa. "I hope I didn't throw it away," she said, rummaging through the clutter in her bag.

No matter how many times she'd helped her mom reorganize her purse, random things still found their way back inside. "What are you looking for?"

She handed Ibelema a crumpled-up receipt with a triumphant smile. "I printed it in case we lost the tracking number."

The receipt was from an electronics store, and Ibelema gasped when she saw the description of the expensive purchase.

"The camera. That was you?"

Mom nodded. "Your dad is so complicated. Instead of just giving it to you for your birthday, he chose the most roundabout way. We had to do a lot just to drop it off at Osagie's office. Even your Aunty didn't know who bought it."

"Dad did that?"

"He said he wanted the best for his girl. And he spent weeks reading reviews, you know how long he takes to buy anything–" She grunted when Ibelema hugged her. "My dear baby."

The tears wouldn't stop. Ibelema hoped they couldn't hear her bawling from the study.

"You deserve the best," Mom said, rubbing her back. "Now is your own time to enjoy."

Ibelema squeezed her eyes shut. Somehow, everything was falling into place.

"Who's that now?" Mom grumbled.

Ibelema sat up and heard the urgent knocking. Someone was at the door.

25

Silas studied the man he desperately needed to impress. He never thought he would be in this position. He'd always thought the father of the woman he wanted to marry would melt like butter in his hands. From his teen years, he'd easily outsmarted seniors, professors, bosses—even his own dad. He was the master of his future and answered to no one, but now, his happiness hung on this one man's decision.

"Your full name is Datonye?" Mr. Pepple asked, and Silas nodded. "God's gift. It's a good name."

Silas swallowed. "Sir, I have something to tell you."

"It's okay. You're sitting here in front of me because you want to do the right thing. I respect that." The older man pinned him in place with his unwavering gaze. "I trust my daughter's judgment. She likes you, so I like you. Whatever you want to say to me, I will listen. Speak freely."

The words should have brought relief, but Silas felt sick instead. "I'm not sure where to begin."

"Start from the beginning."

Silas drew in a deep breath and exhaled, willing himself to not lose his resolve. "First, let me say that I love your daughter. She's everything I prayed for but never thought I could have. I know I don't deserve her, but–"

"Why do you think you don't deserve Ibelema?" His face was hard as stone.

"I guess it's from way back," Silas replied. "I was raised by my dad, and for a long time, I just wanted to prove to myself that I was better than him. I even went to law school just to show him. He was a tough inflexible man, and I blamed him for the hardships of my childhood. We were poor, and when I was young, my mother left us."

His chest felt so tight the words choked him. He took another measured breath to steel his nerves. The older man watched him without saying anything.

"I left law and became an actor in Nigeria," he continued after a beat. "I wanted to make a difference. Thought I could do it my way. But I used people to get ahead, believing the end justified the means. There were women I got involved with, just so I could get connected to the right people."

"You slept with them?"

He nodded, unable to hide his guilt. "There's a scandal right now involving me and a woman. It's the reason I left Nigeria and came to Houston. I'd just starred in this big film as the main lead. At the time, I had stopped going to any parties because I wanted to do something different—I just didn't know what. Every day I just went to work and came straight home."

That was how Silas lived in the months before the scandal.

He'd immersed himself in his craft, developing his acting ability, watching old movies of his favorite actors with days and nights of little food and sleep.

"I was alone at home one night. The gateman was away because of a family tragedy. My bell rang, and my boss' wife was at the door, crying. She looked like someone had hurt her. It was almost midnight, so I brought her inside and called my agent to figure out what to do. The next thing I know, she's jumping on me, begging me not to tell her husband, saying that she wants to be with me and knows how to help me get more roles. I was so angry, I pushed her out on the street."

He glanced at Ibelema's dad and saw that the man was laser-focused on him. "The next day, pictures of us were everywhere, and the headlines called me a home-wrecker, an opportunist, a man-whore—you name it. But I'm telling you sir, I didn't do anything with her. I would never mess around with a married woman. Even when I had lost my way, I still feared God too much."

Mr. Pepple leaned forward, resting a hand on his chin. "And have you found your way now?"

Silas smiled. "Yes, I forgot who I was for a moment, but now, I can see myself well again."

He nodded and pierced Silas with a stern gaze. "I believe you, Datonye."

Silas couldn't breathe. What exactly did the man believe?

"Why do you think you needed to tell me all of this? Because you think I would find out? I can tell you've left nothing out."

Silas rubbed his sweaty palms on his pants. "I...I don't want you to think I'm still that man."

"How could you be? My daughter loves you. She wouldn't love you if you were still that man." Mr. Pepple leaned back in his chair. "Does she know everything?"

Silas shook his head. "Not exactly as I've told you. But I think she does? I mean, most of it is on the internet. And when I tried to tell her, she said it didn't matter."

The older man frowned. "You have to tell her word for word, just like you told me. Women have a way of being swept away in the moment at times, not stopping to fully understand what something means."

"I'll explain everything to her today." He'd intended to get together with her yesterday, but he'd gotten caught up in talking to his dad and the new lawyers hired to help with his case. By the time Silas had wrapped up for the night, it was late and his head was pounding.

Ibelema's dad was staring hard at him. "Why Ibelema? I imagine you've met many women in your life. Why is it my daughter you love?"

The memory came to Silas like a dream. "When I was young, my dad would take me on these fishing trips in Buguma, sometimes at night. I hated those trips. I'd stare into the darkness, waiting for a light to shine in the distance telling us we were close to shore. That's how I felt for a long time in my life, like I was wading in dark waters, not knowing if I'd ever get to the shore."

Silas couldn't help smiling. "Ibelema is like that light to me. She's so bright and beautiful, and I can't help being drawn to her. She's got all these talents and dreams that we need in this world, and I want to be a part of the incredible things she will do. She makes me want to be the best for her, and for myself too. And partnering with her in all she wants to achieve would be the greatest blessing. God sent her to me."

Mr. Pepple's face softened. "You really know how to use words." He laughed, prompting Silas to laugh with him. "Still, from what I've heard, it's clear to me that you need to go back home."

"I plan to." His heart thudded in his chest. Was Ibelema's father rejecting him?

"Right away. You have to go back and fix this mess. Why let your character be continually assaulted? With all you've told me, do you think that as her father, I can be fully comfortable with the two of you together?"

Of course not. As Ibelema's dad, he wouldn't want his only child to be associated with someone who was accused of such vile things. Silas could feel his heart sinking.

Mr. Pepple stood to his feet and gestured for Silas to do the same. "Let's go eat before Ibelema thinks I'm harassing you here." He placed a warm hand on Silas' shoulder. "As I said before, I like you, and nothing has changed. The rest, you and Ibelema will figure it out, my son."

Silas nodded, his eyes stinging with tears, and his chest heaving. Was this what his relationship with his dad would have been like if things had turned out differently with his mom? Unlike his dad, Mr. Pepple seemed happy and accepting. If this was the sort of man who raised Ibelema, then he had a lot of work to do to live up to this standard. He could start by telling her the whole story.

When Silas stepped out of the study with Ibelema's dad, they entered the living room, and Ibelema and her mom came from the kitchen to join them. There was another woman with them, and the woman stayed in the kitchen, staring at him like she'd seen a ghost.

"That was a long talk," Ibelema's mom said, her brows raised. "Are we ready to eat now?"

"Yes, ma'am," Silas replied. "But first, can I talk to Ibelema?"

Her mom chuckled. "Yes. Please talk to her well."

His pulse was racing. "Can we talk outside?"

Ibelema took his hand. "How did it go?" she whispered.

Silas led her out of the house and they stood on the paved path near the garage. "I love you so much," he started, his hands shaking in hers.

The worry on her face melted into a gentle smile. "I love you too, baby."

He squeezed her hands. "But I need to tell you something very important."

"Like right now?" She looked taken aback. "Isn't it a bit too soon?"

"Please, just listen."

The front door opened loudly, and the woman from the kitchen marched toward them, her face twisted in anger. "Get away from her," she shouted, pointing a finger at Silas. Behind her, Ibelema's mom and dad stumbled out.

"Osagie," Mr. Pepple barked. "Go back inside now."

"Brother, I won't." The woman yanked Ibelema away from Silas. "You think I don't know who you are?"

His blood ran cold. This had to be Michael's mother, Aunty Osagie, Mrs. Pepple's younger sister and self-designated bodyguard.

"How dare you touch my Ibelema with your filthy hands?" Her sharp voice echoed through the quiet neighborhood. "Silas Harry, you slimy snake, what are you doing here?"

Ibelema wriggled out of her aunt's grip. "What is wrong with you, Aunty? Please get a hold of yourself."

Her dad pulled the woman away from Ibelema. "Osagie, have you lost your mind? You don't listen to me again? Why are you shouting in the street?"

His rebuke seemed to calm her down. "This is madness, Brother," she insisted. "My sister, why is this Silas Harry in your house trying to marry your daughter?"

"Who is Silas?" Mrs. Pepple asked in confusion. "His name is Tonye."

"Tonye who? Sister, you know him now—we've watched a movie with him in it. This is the actor with the scandal I told you about."

"I'm so sorry," Silas said, his head bowed. One of the closest people to the woman he loved was glaring at him like he was yesterday's trash. He glanced sideways at Ibelema, her eyes swimming in tears.

A defiant Ibelema got in her aunt's face. "I don't know what you think you know, but please stop treating him like this."

"Everyone inside the house," her dad said through clenched teeth.

"We're not going anywhere until someone tells me why this boy—"

"Osagie," Mr. Pepple growled. "Get inside, now."

Aunty Osagie flinched and took a long look at Silas before she stomped away. Mrs. Pepple grabbed Ibelema and dragged her inside against her protests.

Silas stood still, waiting for Mr. Pepple's permission to leave. He couldn't handle everyone looking at him like he was the worst thing that happened to Ibelema. But he wanted to be there by her side and defend himself against the accusation. She needed to hear it from him. He needed to explain everything.

"Please, allow me to—"

"Nothing good will come from you staying here," Mr. Pepple said, raising a hand to silence him. "Don't worry, Ibelema will call you later. Just go home for now." He met Silas' eyes. "Remember, nothing has changed. You told me everything, and I'm on your side."

Silas felt white hot tears rolling down his face. "I'm so sorry," was all he could manage to say.

"It's going to be okay," Ibelema's dad assured him, and walked into the house, the door slamming shut behind him.

26

Ibelema spent the rest of the evening reading about the scandal online, each story worse than the next, though the recently published stories did show that people thought Tonye was set up by the gangster media mogul, and many of the gossip sites were flooded with comments in his defense.

After the spectacle outside, Aunty Osagie pulled up pictures of Tonye–Silas on her phone. "Silas Harry. Disgraced Nollywood Actor. Affair. Homewrecker." A blurred photo of Jeanie Johnson showed the woman leaving his house. There were older pictures of Tonye hanging out with scantily dressed women.

"Why is this happening?" Aunty had wailed. "After that good-for-nothing Kenneth played with you, this new devil appeared to deceive you again."

The words splashed like ice-cold water on Ibelema's face. How could her aunty use that word to describe her kind-hearted

Tonye? He wasn't Kenneth. Sure, Tonye wasn't the typical Christian guy, but he wasn't shifty like them either. Unlike Kenneth, she never had reason to doubt Tonye's love for her. Yet somehow, he was also the same guy in those pictures.

Aunty Osagie had practically jumped Dad when he ordered Ibelema to go upstairs. "You're a smart woman," Dad reminded her. "You have to decide what you will believe."

Mom was fuming. "Why aren't you angry that he tricked us?"

"He told me himself what happened, and I believe him." Dad's eyes never wavered from Ibelema, as if he was only talking to her.

"But all these articles can't be lies," Aunty cried.

"How many times have we read stories and they turned out to be false?" Dad countered. "Ibelema, leave these people and go think for yourself about what you want to do."

"What's there to think about?" Mom snapped. "He lied to us—to Ibelema."

"You don't know that," Dad insisted, turning to Ibelema. "My daughter, the Tonye you know, is he like how they are painting him out to be?"

Ibelema felt numb. She didn't know what to believe. If Tonye had time to tell her dad, why couldn't he tell her first?

She wanted to sleep, but sleep didn't come. Long after she shut herself in her room, she heard the three of them arguing downstairs. Her phone kept vibrating, Tonye calling again and again. She turned off her phone and rubbed her sore eyes.

Against her better judgment, Ibelema scoured more sites and studied more pictures of this Silas Harry. Tonye must have lost weight because Silas was more muscular and clean-shaven. They were the same man, but it was unbelievable how different they looked. But which was actually the real him, Silas or Tonye?

"God, I don't know what to think." Somehow, Ibelema drifted off as she was praying.

When she woke up, it was around six in the morning. The house was eerily quiet despite the birds chirping outside. Her head was throbbing. She turned on her phone to find 10 voicemails, most of them from Tonye. Her heart broke at his desperate voice begging her to call him back so he could explain everything.

Barbara and Kay left two voicemails as well. She was tempted to call them back. They knew about the scandal and never told her.

Ibelema put her phone down and went downstairs. Reading more gossip wasn't helping anything. She needed to take a walk. Dad would have already left for work, so she would only have Mom to deal with. Hopefully no one was home. She couldn't handle their questions or bear the pity in their eyes.

Her steps halted as Dad walked out of the study, and her eyes welled with tears. Why was he home at this time?

"You didn't go to work?"

"I was waiting for you," Dad said. "Will you walk with me?"

After some hesitation, she accepted his outstretched hand. As they strolled around the neighborhood, Ibelema tried to remember when last they went together. Dad usually didn't like walking with her or Mom because they "walked too slowly," but today, he seemed in no hurry to leave her behind, his hand clutching hers. It was sweet. She almost laughed when a young couple eyed them curiously as they jogged past.

For some time, Dad said nothing, and she didn't feel rushed to speak either. A comfortable silence stretched between them as the bullfrogs and cicadas croaked their morning songs. The sun rose high above the curtain of trees fencing the greenbelt in their quiet neighborhood. The air thick with fog, a light breeze kissed her face.

Why was she acting like she had any choice in this? She was in love with the man. She owed it to herself to call him back and hear what he had to say.

"Have you thought about what you want?" Dad finally spoke. They'd made it to the other side of their subdivision, but he showed no signs of letting go of her hand.

Ibelema shook her head. What happened to the man who usually told her what she should want? She stared at her father, wishing he would just tell her what to do, or give her a reason to do what she already knew she would end up doing. After a lifetime of never knowing what it meant to fall in love, how could she not take this gamble?

Dad smiled up at the blue and orange sky. "Remember when you wanted to be an artist? You used to paint the sky in different colors. Sometimes, your sky was red and purple."

Ibelema managed to smile at him. Middle school was a weird time for her.

"I never understood how a sky could be red and purple until I saw it one day when jogging. After that, I always wished to see it again because it was so beautiful." His casual tone belied the depth of his words. "You've taught me many things, my precious one. Sometimes it takes me a while, but seeing the world through your eyes has given me great joy."

Ibelema stopped in her tracks. She had known him all her life and still couldn't understand him. He was a walking contradiction. Were all men that way? He'd harassed her to become a nurse and settle down, so what exactly was he trying to say now?

Dad released her hand and placed his weathered hands on her shoulders. "You've always been perceptive and wiser than your years. Even when you were a baby, I felt as if you understood what was going on. You'd quietly watch and listen, weighing and pondering what to do. And once you acted, whether I liked it or not, you made your choice and stuck to it."

Ibelema didn't recognize the person he described. "I'm not that person anymore."

"I know." He cringed as though in pain. "I want to apologize to you. My expectations have not only inhibited your gifts but silenced your voice. Clouded your judgment."

Was he talking about her failure to recognize Tonye's double life? Or that she could never decide on what career path to pursue and had settled for nursing?

"From now on, your mother and I promise to support you in whatever decision you make."

Her eyes went misty with fresh tears of frustration. Usually, Dad imposed his opinion on her, and now when she needed it most, he wanted to sit back and watch. "But I don't know what to do."

He squeezed her shoulders. "You do. I trust your judgment, Ibelema. Always have."

"Why? I always screw things up." Falling in love that fast was naive. "How can you trust that I'm doing the right thing? I don't even trust myself not to make the same mistakes."

"That's part of life. What you have to understand is you're not the same person you were just yesterday." Dad brushed her cheek and smiled. "Have you forgotten who you are? Do you think that God will let you fail, you who want so much to please Him?"

Wasn't she failing already? No job, no real future, and on top of that, the man she loved wasn't who she thought he was.

Dad wrapped his arms around her. "You have your whole life

ahead of you. It's time to stop second-guessing what you already know to be true." Ibelema leaned her head against his chest, and Dad stroked her back. "Listen, then act."

"Are we talking about Tonye or something else?"

"Your film, your dreams, Tonye—everything. We will support whatever decision you make. No matter what that is."

Ibelema's heart ached at the tender look on Dad's face. He'd talked with Tonye, so he wouldn't be saying all this right now if he didn't believe him.

"I need to see him." She needed to hear Tonye and see if what she knew was a lie.

His mouth twitched, clearly amused. "Then go see him."

"What did he tell you? Why do you believe him?"

"I don't know about his Nigeria trouble, but when I talked to him, I felt he was a man who would do right by you." Dad smiled. "So, go hear for yourself and decide if what he did is more than you can accept."

"Accept?"

"Are you angry because you believe he did what they said he did?"

"No." That wasn't it. He hadn't trusted her enough to tell her about the scandal. Or tried to make her understand what she was getting into. He had many chances to make her really understand the situation.

"Love is more than butterflies and romance," Dad said softly. "It's also acceptance and forgiveness."

Ibelema looked down at a small frog leaping along the sidewalk onto the grass. "And you're not just saying this because he's your townsman?"

Dad made a face, feigning shock at her accusation. "He's your townsman too."

"All this support you're talking about has me scared. Are you sure this is what Mom agreed to?"

He laughed. "You know how she is. Let's just pretend that's what she said."

She put her arms around him, and together they walked back to their side of the neighborhood. "Thanks, Dad."

She knew what she had to do. Now, she just needed the courage to do it.

27

His call went straight to voicemail again, Ibelema's sweet voice mocking him. This wasn't how it was meant to go. He barely got any sleep last night, and he hadn't eaten since yesterday morning.

He could smell the spices as he walked up the scenic path to the house. He didn't have to knock because Efe opened the door with a bright smile. She seemed to hesitate before hugging him. It would take a while for both of them to get used to having a sibling.

Silas had called earlier to ask if it was okay for him to come over. If he was going to convince Ibelema to trust him, making up with his mother was a must.

Efe led him to the living room where their mother was waiting with a nervous smile. Silas went up to her, hesitating before wrapping her in a careful hug. He had challenged himself to do so the next time he saw her, and it wasn't as hard as he thought it would be.

His mother stood stiff for a second, and when her arms enclosed him in a tighter embrace, it was his turn to tell himself to relax. He didn't expect it to feel so good, being hugged by the woman he had wondered about all these years. By the time he released her, she was crying.

"Thank you," his mom sniffed through her tears.

Efe had tears in her eyes too. "I'll leave you guys alone."

"No, please stay." It would be more awkward with her gone. "I wanted to talk to you too."

Efe looked happy as she sat down on the couch. His mom offered him something to eat, but Silas declined. His youngest sister wasn't back from high school. Efe's dad was working late.

"Can I see pictures of her?" Silas asked.

Efe showed him pictures of their little sister on her phone, then pulled out several photo albums. Their mom watched from a distance, like she was unsure how to act in this new dynamic.

"I'm sorry for ignoring you for so long," Silas said.

She stared at him with her mouth open. "You have nothing to apologize for. I'm just glad you're here, and that you get to meet your sisters." Her eyes were teary again.

His phone ringing in his pocket made him jerk. Thinking it was Ibelema, he almost picked up but decided against it. He couldn't talk to his dad right now.

"Is it IB?" Efe asked.

Silas shook his head and rejected the call. His mom smiled at him, probably guessing it was his dad on the line.

"Is everything ok with IB?" Efe scooted closer to Silas on the couch.

His heart shattered all over again. What if Ibelema no longer wanted anything to do with him? She hadn't replied to any of his texts since yesterday. Barbara had scolded him on the phone because she was even ignoring them too.

"Are you okay, Tonye?" his mom asked in the softest voice.

Silas nodded. "Efe, have you talked to IB today?"

"No, she hasn't replied to my last text."

"She's mad at me," Silas admitted. "Something bad happened back home that I should have told her about."

Efe groaned. "I knew it. You didn't tell her at all? Tonye, that's not cool."

The way Efe was looking at him, she had to know. "When did you find out?"

"Some weeks back," Efe replied.

"And you didn't say anything?"

"To IB? God, no. I knew she'd trip, IB can be very extra. I figured you'd tell her once we were done shooting." She cast Silas a disappointed look. "I guess not."

"I'm sorry," he said, a little unnerved by the strange new feeling of letting his sister down. This big brother thing was going to be complicated.

Efe sighed. "So, what did she say when she found out?"

His phone buzzed. Silas checked it and shot up from the couch. He wanted to shout. Finally, a reply. A link with directions to a park. *Meet me here*, her text read.

"That's her. I have to go." He hugged Efe and their mom. The park wasn't far away, but the rush-hour traffic was bad.

When Silas finally got to the park, he practically sprinted across the wooden bridge. He didn't see Ibelema at first in the open field, but he found her standing by a memorial bench at the edge of the park.

His heart beat faster as he walked toward her. Dark circles

colored her brown eyes, meaning she hadn't been sleeping well either. Beautiful and sad, Ibelema stood with her arms wrapped around herself as if she were cold.

He wanted to hug her but curled his fingers into his palms. "How long were you waiting?"

Her red-rimmed eyes searched him, and she drew in a shaky breath. When he stepped forward, she raised her hands to stop him from coming close.

"Ibelema, I am so sorry."

"For what? What are you sorry for?"

The disappointment in her voice stabbed him. Whenever a woman asked that question, it was a trap. What did she want him to say? He just needed to tell it like it was.

"I'm sorry because I didn't trust you with the truth."

That seemed to be what she wanted to hear. Her face softened and she let out a loud breath.

"I'm sorry it took me so long to tell you. I made you look bad in front of your family."

Ibelema let out a strangled laugh. "That's an understatement."

"You're right. I should have told you from the start."

Her eyes chilled him. "The fact that you know exactly what you did wrong is what scares me the most. How do I know you're not playing me right now?"

The accusation felt like a punch to his gut. Why did she sound so cold? Had her dad told her everything?

"I'm sorry I hurt you, and there's no reason I can give. But I'm telling you the truth now. I never tried to play you, I just–"

"I feel like I don't know you," she choked out. "The man I thought I knew would never run away without a fight. How could you let them spread lies about you like that?"

Silas stepped back from her, smiling in spite of himself. Instead of asking him questions, Ibelema was challenging his decision to run away.

"I'm going to sue them," he announced.

She didn't look impressed. "How can you effectively fight them from here?" Her quiet voice made his chest ache in anticipation of the dreaded words. "You're not supposed to be here right now."

"I'm innocent, Ibelema."

"Not completely. You let her in, Tonye. There's no way you didn't know that woman had feelings for you."

His voice caught in his throat. She was right. "I'm an actor. Women come on to me all the time. She was my boss' wife and she was crying and–"

"I can't believe I'm having this conversation with the man I want to marry."

"I'm still the same man," Silas insisted. He still had a chance. Calm down, he told himself. She still wanted to marry him. "I didn't do any of the things they said."

"That's not the point." Ibelema paced in front of him, looking angrier by the second. "You sold your soul to that evil man for your career, then you let them put dump on your name and call you a homewrecker."

Hearing her recall the scandal from her sweet mouth hurt more than he'd expected. He had known she would research everything once she found out. In her eyes, the issue wasn't whether he slept with that woman or not—it was that he'd gotten wrapped up with someone like Johnson to begin with.

She paused her frantic pacing to close the gap between them. "Look at me." Her hands framed his face and drew his eyes down to hers. "The man I love wouldn't do those things. But the man I love did take a long time to tell me the whole truth, even though he could say pretty words like 'I love you' so easily."

Silas couldn't bear to see the disappointment in her face and wanted to avert his eyes, but her hands stayed him in place. Ibelema still loved him, but it almost sounded like she couldn't move past what happened.

"Instead of introducing you to my parents as the man I've chosen, I had to hear about you being a womanizer. And don't get me started on the fact that I can't even figure out what to call you right now."

"Whatever you want to call me," he croaked, helpless. "You know who I am."

She looked at him as if he had a point. "Not Silas Harry. I don't like him. He's having an identity crisis, and he seems unstable with no direction. It's hard to reconcile him with the Tonye I know." She shook her head violently. "And your agent needs to be fired. It's obvious he doesn't have your best interest. Half of those dramas he booked you have nothing to do with anything. They take so long to get going that by the time 'Silas' shows up, I forget what I'm watching."

Silas reached for her hand as she spoke, but Ibelema sidestepped his reach, stretching the distance between them. Her eyes were dark, the accusatory glint in them like a vacuum sucking all the hope out of him. She was building a case to break things off with him. He was desperate to be with her, but Ibelema just wanted to move on.

"How could you run away because of a lie?" Ibelema went on. "What about all the things you're meant to do? Many young people back home depend on you, and you're here doing what exactly?"

His throat was sore. "I was planning on going back soon, next week. I already talked to my dad and made arrangements."

"Then go." Her eyes shone with unshed tears. "Go home. Goodbye, Tonye."

She turned on her heels to walk away from him, but Silas grabbed her arm and whirled her around. "What about us? Why do I have to let you go?"

"Because it's better this way," she said, yanking her hand away.

Silas stumbled in front of her and wrapped his arms around her, tightening his hold as she tried to push him away.

"You're the best thing that's ever happened to me," he said in a quiet voice.

"Likewise," she whispered, tears rolling down.

If only he had met her before all this. "Then why are you leaving me?"

She sniffed back her tears in his embrace. "Who knows? You might end up being the worst thing that's ever happened to me. How am I supposed to fall in love again after loving you?"

Silas held on tight. "God Himself would have to kill me before I let you go."

"Don't say things like that."

"Then give me another chance." His voice sounded pathetic even in his ears. "I'll fix this. Whatever you want me to do, whatever you want me to be, I'll do it. Just don't leave me."

Ibelema stopped struggling in his arms. "Tonye, you have to take care of this before we can think of moving forward. It's the only way we have a chance."

"I know, but Nigerian courts are complicated. This thing can take a long time." He couldn't imagine being without her for a month, talk less of a year or more. "I can't leave you. Don't you love me anymore?"

"I just told you I did. But that's not–"

"Then come with me." The words escaped before he knew what he said. She gaped at him like he was asking the impossible. How could he ask her to leave her life, her family and everything she knew to come with him? He knew it was a long shot, but he had no other choice.

"I know I'm asking a lot. I'm being selfish right now, and I hate that I'm doing this to you. But I don't see how I'm supposed to live another day without you, Ibelema. I can't do it, I just can't, not when I love you more than my own life."

She looked like she was trying to hold back her tears, but they trickled down her cheeks anyway. "You're not being fair."

Silas stroked her hair, wondering what he would do if he never got to hold her like this again. "Sorry, but I'm fighting for my life here."

"And what about my life?"

"I'm fighting for yours too." He pressed her close to him. "No one can make you happier than me, my love. Let's do this together, all those things we talked about. Let's get married and help change our country. Please, come with me."

28

"I'm so sorry, IB," Barbara pleaded, her big eyes round with remorse. Barbara had shown up at Shoot Me Studios with sandwiches for the editing team as a peace offering. "What else can I do to make this up to you?"

Ibelema eyed her friend. She wasn't angry with Barbara anymore. Part of her understood why they didn't tell her. If she knew the truth, she would never have given Tonye a chance, and she was glad she did. Still, after all that happened, he was asking her to drop her whole life and go to Nigeria with him?

Ibelema hugged Barbara in the parking lot. "We're good. Did he tell Kay what he asked me?"

Barbara nodded, biting her lip. "IB, that's...."

Tonye had gazed at her with those disarming puppy eyes and asked her to think about it, but she didn't want to entertain the thought. She didn't belong in Nigeria, hadn't stepped foot in that country since high school, when she'd visited some relatives for a few weeks. How did Tonye expect her to navigate that scary place while he resolved his scandal? Plus, if she went with him, the spotlight would be on her.

Ibelema looked up and saw Daniel at the office doors. He gestured to her and walked back inside.

"They need me." She waved to Barbara, promising to call her later.

Austin and Elliot had set up a meeting to talk about the film's edits. Seated in their office, Ibelema struggled to pay attention until she heard Tonye's name.

"What was that about Tonye?" Ibelema asked.

Austin exchanged glances with Daniel. "Tonye paid for the edits," Daniel explained.

Ibelema sighed. Of course he did. Hearing about his latest act of support only made her more annoyed. Tonye had inserted himself into her life so easily that she couldn't go a day without hearing his name.

Once they signed a few documents, Ibelema left with Daniel. "I still can't believe you knew who he was and didn't tell me," Ibelema said. Earlier on, when she'd told Daniel what happened with Tonye, he hadn't even blinked.

"We needed to finish the project," Daniel said. "And no one believes he did what they said he did."

"That's not the point."

"No. But is there really a good time to bring up something like that, especially when he's being accused of something he didn't do?"

Ibelema wanted to smack the back of his head. She hated talking to Daniel sometimes—he made her see reason where she wanted to see none. She didn't want to tell him about the going to

Nigeria part because she knew what he would say. God, even she was starting to know what she should say. But it was nuts just imagining it.

"So, what do you think of him?"

Daniel's brows lifted. "Tonye, or Silas Harry?"

Ibelema scoffed. "I keep forgetting who I'm talking to."

"Are you confused they might be the same person?"

As usual, Daniel had seen right through her. "They are," she replied. "Kind of. Aren't I allowed to be confused?"

He seemed to think about it. "It feels like you're looking for a reason to be, and I can't help you with that. Have you talked to Kimani?"

After Ibelema's walk with her dad around the subdivision, she had called Kimani and told her everything. They talked again yesterday, and she had expected her usually reasonable friend to talk her out of thinking about Nigeria. She couldn't deny she loved the man, no matter how frustrating the situation, but was love enough to overcome the inevitable drama awaiting them in their immediate future? Uprooting her life for someone who hadn't thought to trust her wasn't the logical move to make, yet even Kimani seemed to agree that maybe going to Nigeria wasn't the worst thing that could happen.

Her phone rang. Pastor Luke wanted to know if she could stop by the church.

"I'll head over now," Ibelema told him, saying goodbye to Daniel and heading to church. She played some worship music in her car, but it didn't help settle her thoughts. Tonye was leaving for Nigeria next week. Maybe he could go home and sort his mess out, then come back so they could pick up where they left off and get married. The only problem was how long that would take. Could she go months without seeing him? A long-distance relationship on top of everything else sounded like the worst possible path to take.

When Ibelema entered the church office lobby, she ran into the last person she needed to see, almost hissing a bad word at her rotten luck. She walked past him with a fake smile.

"Wait," Kenneth called.

"I have to see Pastor Luke."

"He's talking to someone else right now."

She kept walking until he grabbed her hand, and she glared at him until he released her.

"That guy in your film is a no-good actor from Nigeria," Kenneth declared.

"Excuse me?" He was talking about Tonye too?

"They say he sexually assaulted a woman back home."

Ibelema shook her head feverishly as if to banish the devil. All the anger of the past months descended on her like a fiery shower.

"First of all, get your facts straight. He didn't sexually assault anyone or do any of those things they're saying."

"It's all over the internet."

"And that makes it true?"

"You need to stop deceiving yourself."

She couldn't believe this fool. "Get lost, Kenneth. You don't need to worry yourself about me and my fiancé."

"Fiancé?" He nearly shouted the word, then looked around, but there was no one else in the lobby. His face twisted, and his breath grew ragged. "Okay, sorry. This isn't how I wanted this talk to go." She started to walk away, and Kenneth grabbed her hand again but let go at once.

"Please just listen to me. I made a mistake, okay?" He dragged his hand across his forehead. "I'm breaking off the engagement with Ruth."

"You're what?" Wait, how was this any of her business? Ibelema turned to go.

"Please, don't marry that devil," he pleaded. "You're more than that."

"Screw you, Kenneth—you're the devil."

"I love you, IB."

That made her stop. Those words coming out of his mouth sounded all wrong. She looked over her shoulder at him. His face was sad, desperate. After how he treated her, he dared to look that way and think his words would hold any weight?

"I can't marry another woman when I'm in love with you."

"You don't love me. You never did."

"I did—I do. I was just under so much pressure. My parents and Pastor—I mean, people—warned me that you weren't wife material because your head is in the clouds. But that's exactly why I love you. You're not like any other woman I know."

She felt the fire burning through her veins. His parents? Was that what they thought of her? Kenneth had said "Pastor" as if he was going to call a name. She was about to ask who when she saw fear flash in his eyes. Pastor Luke was standing at the other end of the lobby with none other than Ruth herself.

Ibelema stalked toward them. She thought maybe they didn't hear Kenneth, but Ruth's face instantly crumpled. The pastor grabbed Ruth's arm, but Ruth yanked her hand free and marched toward the frozen Kenneth.

"I see you're still trying to steal my husband," Ruth hissed as she passed Ibelema.

"Girl, please. You sound ridiculous."

Pastor Luke looked like he wanted to run away from the scene. He waved Ibelema toward the office, and she didn't bother looking back at the unhappy couple. They deserved each other. If she had her way, she'd never lay eyes on them again.

Once they entered the safety of his office, Pastor Luke sighed. "That was...awkward."

Ibelema didn't trust herself to speak. She didn't want to be here, didn't want to chance running into Kenneth or Ruth again. Efe was right. Even though this was the only church she'd ever known, she couldn't stay here any longer. Kenneth's parents had known her since she was a baby, so why would they say that about her? And who were the other pastors?

"Are you okay?" Pastor Luke asked.

She glared at him, waiting for him to explain why he wanted to see her at the same time that Ruth and Kenneth just happened to be here.

He fidgeted with some papers on his desk, and when he met Ibelema's eyes again, he looked more nervous.

Then it hit her.

"Was it you?"

"Was it me what?" Pastor Luke asked, without looking at her.

"Did you tell Kenneth not to marry me?"

His eyes widened. "Is that what he said?" When she didn't respond, he laughed. "Kenneth's going through a lot right now, so don't pay attention to him."

Pastor Luke cleared his throat. "Actually, I called you here to offer you a job as the Ministry Creative Director for our whole church. We created this position specifically for you, so that you can use your God-given gifts here with us. As Creative Director, you'd be given freedom to create anything that benefits our church, whether it's more films, youth dramas, songwriting, or the inner-city projects we have planned, whatever your spirit is leading you to do. But you also have a place on the worship team.

The pay's pretty good, and you'll get your own office. You just have to go through two interviews, and the job is yours. You've earned it, IB."

Ibelema's jaw dropped. She couldn't believe how long she'd waited to hear those words. Ministry Creative Director was better than she ever expected, a position created just for her after all the time she'd put in. She would have the church's backing for more films, and wouldn't be as restricted as the other members of the worship team.

Ibelema almost laughed at the turn of events, not because she was happy to finally be rewarded, but because the offer came at the worst possible time. And now, she felt dead inside looking at the man she once thought of as her mentor.

"So, I'm finally good enough to be on staff, but was never good enough to be Kenneth's wife?" Ibelema scoffed.

Pastor Luke frowned. "What are we talking about here? I just offered you a job even better than the job you've always wanted."

"Please, answer the question." Her voice was so cold it surprised her.

He adjusted his collar. "What do you want me to say, IB?"

She suddenly wanted to get as far away from here as possible, so she stood to her feet. "Pastor Luke, I don't want anything from you. But thanks for everything." She marched out of his office and didn't dare look back even when he called her name.

In the lobby, Ruth and Kenneth were arguing. As Ibelema rushed out of the building, someone called her name again, but she didn't stop to see if it was Kenneth or Pastor Luke. What a crazy day this was turning out to be.

Once Ibelema got into her car, her phone made her jump, and she shouted his name in wonder. Her Tonye was calling. What sort of perfect timing did he have? She could almost hear his voice telling her he was proud of her, that she deserved much better than these people at her church.

Tears rolled down her cheeks. She just wanted to talk to him, to see his face and kiss him, his eyes sparkling with pride and love.

Ibelema let out a chuckle and shook her head. "Who am I kidding?" It was just like the song. How was she supposed to live without him?

She started to call him back, then thought of something else that made her smile. She dialed her mom's number. Mom picked up at first ring.

"Mommy, are you and Daddy home? I need to talk to you both."

"We're here." It was her dad's voice. He sounded like he already knew what she wanted to discuss.

Through her rearview mirror, Ibelema saw a wild-eyed Kenneth stumble out of the church building with Ruth and Pastor Luke on his heels.

"I'm on my way now," Ibelema said, reversing out of the parking spot. She swerved around Kenneth and headed straight home, leaving the three of them behind.

29

Silas fiddled with the pair of one-way plane tickets in his hand. He looked behind him again at the busy traffic in the airport. Two months ago, he'd arrived alone with one black suitcase, and now he was returning the same way.

"Just the one bag?" asked the woman at the counter.

"Yeah." He swallowed his hopeful "for now" as he looked back at the doors leading out of the airport.

"I hope you enjoyed your visit," the airport employee said, typing on her keyboard. "I've heard Houston's not that much different from Lagos, weather-wise."

"I guess," he replied, careful to keep his tone polite despite his nerves.

She stopped typing and gave him a sort of confidential smile. "I'm Nigerian too, but I've never gone back there. Been meaning to visit but can't bring myself to actually do it."

Silas nodded in understanding. "Sometimes you just have to take a leap."

"I know, right? One of my friends packed all her stuff and moved to Lagos after college." She shook her head, his luggage check-in forgotten. "She did youth service and everything, and she's doing well now. Still, I can't imagine leaving everything to go stay in a place where I don't really know anyone."

Silas felt like he'd swallowed an egg. Her story sounded too familiar. "But you have your friend," he managed to reply.

"It's not the same as having family there. It's so scary, I couldn't do it." She resumed typing his information. "Please give me a minute. I'm having some technical issues here."

"No problem." Listening to this woman, Silas realized how selfish he must have sounded. When he talked to Ibelema yesterday, she told him everything was going to be okay, and they wouldn't be apart for as long as he thought.

"You don't seem happy to be going home," the woman piped up again.

Silas smiled. "The way you pick up on stuff, you must be Nigerian."

She put a hand over her mouth to stifle her laugh. "Sorry."

"It's okay. I'm just leaving someone special behind, that's all." What was home without Ibelema?

"Your wife?"

"No, my girlfriend."

"You should have taken her with you then."

"She didn't want to come."

"That's probably because you haven't asked her to marry you yet."

"Actually, I did ask her."

She looked invested. "What did she say?"

"I'm not sure. She didn't say no, exactly."

"Very interesting." The woman handed him his passport and placed his bag on the conveyor belt. "Well, you're good to go, sir. I hope everything works out for you." Her smile widened and she pointed behind him. "Could that be your girlfriend over there looking at you?"

Silas whirled around. At first, he thought he was seeing things. Ibelema was standing outside the lined area. It really was her. Silas closed the gap between them in a flash and took her in his arms, but his heart dropped when he saw she had no luggage with her.

"Did...you come to see me off?"

"I came," Ibelema said, without cracking a smile.

He had purchased two tickets last minute, hoping he could convince her. But now Silas understood he'd only thought of himself. Still, he couldn't form the words. Goodbye wasn't something he was prepared to say, not to Ibelema. His chest felt like it was being ripped apart.

"Are you ready?" Ibelema's voice jerked him back to his desperate reality.

He shook his head. "I don't think I can leave you."

She tilted her head to look at him. "Why would you leave me?"

He tried to understand. "But you said..."

"What did I say?"

He searched her eyes, surprised to see that she looked a little annoyed. "It wasn't fair me asking you to drop everything and come with me," he said, trying not to offend her again.

"You think?" She smiled. "But I forgive you. That's why I'm here." She raised one hand, waving a small blue book between her fingers.

As the realization dawned on him that she was holding a passport, Silas' heart jumped into his throat, and he choked out a gasp. Tears crowded his eyes. He buried his face in her neck, kissed her skin and breathed her in. He had missed her flowery smell.

"How could I let you leave without me, silly?" Ibelema chuckled. "We're in this together."

"Thank you," Silas whispered, trying to will the tears away. "Thank you, my love."

Ibelema drew back and held his face between her palms. "I love you, Tonye Silas Banigo." She leaned in to kiss him. "I choose you. Always."

Silas cupped the back of her neck and kissed her with all of the relief, excitement and gratitude he was feeling. Every day away from Ibelema had felt like torture. But now she was coming with him, forever.

Ibelema reared back as if she had forgotten something. "But first, there's a little thing we need to do. To fulfill all righteousness, you know?"

Silas bobbed his head. "Anything you want."

"Let's get married."

"Of course we will." Tomorrow he'd look for the biggest diamond for her engagement ring.

"Right now," she went on. "I can't get on this plane unless we get married."

He blinked, waiting for her to smile like he was being punked. She shoved a small box into his right hand. Silas opened it, blinking when he realized that there was a ring inside.

"Come on. Ask me to marry you again."

"I don't think–"

"Don't think, just say the words."

She looked so serious he did as he was told. "Ibelema, from the moment I saw you–"

"Skip to the good part. I have to check in too."

"Oh, okay," he stammered, and took a deep breath. "Ibelema, my love, will you marry me?"

"Yes," she cried, her eyes bright.

As Silas slipped the ring on her finger, people started clapping around them. He had forgotten they were in the airport.

"Here they come," Ibelema nudged him. "Our witnesses."

Ibelema's parents were walking over with Kimani and an engaged couple he'd met at Phoebe's wedding. Behind them, Barbara carried Tiwa while Kay and Daniel dragged two suitcases along. And last of all, Efe and his mom were holding hands with tears in their eyes.

"What's this?" Silas asked, trying to find the words.

Ibelema grinned widely like a Cheshire cat. "I can have secrets too, my love."

Silas would have laughed if he wasn't so confused. He hugged her dad and mom, who looked a little worried, but smiled at him and patted his cheek.

"Happy for you, big bro." An excited Efe threw her arms around him, and then it was his mom's turn to hug him.

Kay slapped Silas' back. "Congrats, my guy. We're here to make it official."

"You're getting married," Barbara cheered in a sing-song voice, bouncing Tiwa on her hip.

"You remember Judah and Tari," Ibelema said, pointing at the couple. "Judah's going to marry us."

"Wait o," Mrs. Pepple said with a frown. "I didn't see anyone kneeling down yet."

"Mom, we're in a hurry." Ibelema threw her a long look.

Silas caught Mr. Pepple's eyes, and the older man nodded in approval. Silas dropped to his knees and waited for Ibelema to meet his eyes.

"My Sugar in Sugar Land, you're everything I want but never deserved. The greatest treasure I've ever found, I promise to always honor you as the best of me as we walk this journey of life together. So, please, be my lady, my wife. Ibelema Pepple, will you marry me?"

Her eyes danced. "Yes, I'll marry you."

Silas jumped to his feet and grabbed her, the entire terminal cheering around them.

Ibelema's mom nodded with a satisfied smile. "Okay, Pastor Judah. Do your work."

Silas and Ibelema faced Judah, and Silas glanced around the airport, wondering why no one was trying to stop them. Instead, his fellow travelers were all smiles, and some people even had teary eyes. His new Nigerian friend at the counter gave him two thumbs up.

"I never thought I would ever be doing this in an airport," Judah said, and everyone laughed. "Tonye, do you take this woman as your wife before God and man?"

Silas held her hands. "I do. I always will."

"And Ibelema, do you take this man as your husband before God and man?"

Her cheeks rounded in that adorable way he loved so much. "Always," she said. "I do."

Silas couldn't wait. He leaned in to kiss her, and remembering where they were, stopped midway.

"It's not yet time, *abeg*," Ibelema's mom protested with a laugh.

"By the power invested in me by the state of Texas, I now

pronounce you husband and wife. Now you may kiss your bride."

Silas pulled Ibelema close to him. "I'll give you the best wedding you want—a traditional wedding too." He kissed her lips, her cheeks, her forehead. "I promise to make you the happiest woman ever."

"But first, you have to make me very happy tonight," she whispered in his ear.

Silas pulled back in shock. "I don't need to promise that, Mrs. Banigo. I can do that in my sleep."

Ibelema giggled. "I'll hold you to that, Mr. IB."

Silas threw back his head in a hearty laugh. He was hopelessly in love with her, and he couldn't wait for tonight.

Bonus Chapter

Tonye woke up with a start. The room was dark, and the air felt different. His hand searched the empty spot beside him. He'd dreamed the most beautiful dream, but Ibelema wasn't there on the bed.

He got up and went in search of his wife, finding her on the balcony, with the slate gray sky behind her lovely silhouette. His heart skipped just looking at her. She was more beautiful every day. Her hair was loose around her shoulders, her skin kissed by the soft light as she looked out at the skyline.

"How did I get so lucky?" Tonye whispered. Would he ever get used to seeing her every time he opened his eyes?

Ibelema looked over her shoulder with her infectious smile. "Why are you just standing there?"

"Because I'll take you back to bed if I don't." Her cheeky grin weakened his resolve to give her some breathing room. He felt like he'd been on top of her since they got back from the last film festival where she'd won her third award of the season. They hadn't won anything at the TIFF Festival last year, but A Week on the Mountain got so much hype that many correctly predicted that the stunning Nigerian director was on her way to becoming a household name.

"Are you okay?" he asked.

"There's something so idyllic about Port Harcourt, though it's amazing how similar it is to Lagos, even NEPA."

Tonye turned toward the door. "Let me check why they haven't put on the generator."

"No, just come here." She held out her hand to him. "Don't be shy."

"Me? Shy?" He palmed her hair, teased by the wind, and wrapped an arm around her. Since buying this house last October, they'd spent many nights out here on the balcony, gazing into the horizon until the sun rose above the jagged skyline.

Ibelema leaned into him, and he marveled at how perfectly they fit together. He pressed a soft kiss on her temple, and her flowery scent engulfed his senses. What an intoxicating woman. Making love to her was the best experience of his entire life.

"I feel like I'm in a dream," he said aloud. The past year had been unreal, as if God was working overtime. There was no way he could ever explain finding himself in her world, falling in love with her, having her fall in love with him, then bringing her back to his world.

When they arrived in Lagos more than a year ago, it was pure madness. Though the news of the missing school girls had swiftly replaced his scandal, Tonye had taken interview after interview as the masses swung to his side. People loved Ibelema. She was hailed as the next big director and went on several interviews alongside him, which did wonders for his image.

Maxwell Johnson was still missing, and Jeanie Johnson had fled Nigeria for Dubai. Tonye fired Ejiro after the agent proved to be every bit as shady as Dad said. Then they focused on bringing Tonye Banigo the philanthropist to the forefront while relegating Silas Harry to the sidelines.

Before he knew it, the pathway opened to politics, a pleasant surprise for his dad, who had been laying the foundation for years. Tonye's name was on everyone's lips, and in less than a year, he went from being unknown to actually having a decent chance at the House.

Last December, they traveled back to America for their wedding. Tonye had promised Ibelema a proper wedding, and that was what he delivered, a traditional and church wedding just days apart. They got married in front of her family and friends, and his parents saw each other for the first time in 15 years. Then he took Ibelema on a real honeymoon to Bali.

When they returned to Nigeria, the campaign dominated their lives. In March, Tonye had won by a slim margin and was sworn into the House.

Now, as they stood on the balcony with their whole lives ahead of them, Tonye wondered if she was happy.

"This past year has felt like a movie," Ibelema agreed. "I couldn't have written a better script."

Tonye leaned in close, breathing her in. She smelled so good. He nipped the skin below her ear.

"What do you think happens next?" she asked.

Hopefully, it involved getting her back to bed. "You tell me, my lovely wife."

"Wife." Ibelema practically sang the word. "I love hearing you say that word."

He kissed her neck. "What else do you love?"

"How you touch me, and need me."

She turned to him with an attractive blush. He met her lips in response, peppering kisses on her chin, along her jawline, and down to the nape of her neck, feeling her racing pulse against his mouth. His hands trailed to her small waist, the alluring curve of her hips, the swell of her shapely behind that felt as good as it looked in anything she wore.

"Do you have any idea how much I love you?" She felt like heaven in his arms and tasted as sweet as her name.

Her fingers traced his lips. "I think I do."

"You fearless woman, how could you be so brave to come here with me? Weren't you afraid it was such bad timing?"

"Whether it was the right timing or not, it's our timing, so we're going to make it work," Ibelema said with an air of finality.

Her firm but softly spoken words warmed his blood. He would just have to show her how grateful he was for her love, her trust. Just like that older lady back in Austin did for her husband, Ibelema had left her world for his. Was this the sort of fierce love they'd talked about?

"I don't deserve you, sugar."

"I'm here. And I'm yours." She flashed him another cheeky grin, her brown eyes twinkling with promise. "Just continue to make every night as wonderful as last night."

Enough talk. Her sultry tone was driving him wild. Tonye lifted her in his arms, silencing her protests with soft kisses as he shut their bedroom door.

He couldn't tear himself away from her until hours later. He left home late for his meeting with a benefactor. Arriving at the classy restaurant, Tonye was shown to a private room, but the old gentleman he was meeting wasn't alone.

"Hakeem," Tonye mumbled. Last he'd heard, Hakeem Musa had married his girlfriend Geri in the most lavish ceremony Abuja had seen in years. Hakeem had sent him an invitation, but Tonye never thought to attend, though the invite had reminded him about Bart Teka back in Houston. He kept forgetting to ask his dad about Bart. Since Bart was adopted and didn't know his parents, maybe his dad could look into it.

Tonye's benefactor pushed back from his chair. "I'll leave you two so you can talk."

When the old man left the room, Hakeem let out a deep breath. "Tonye, I know we're not on the best of terms but I need your help."

Tonye kept a straight face. Since he'd become a Representative, people were always asking him for favors. But what could he have that Hakeem needed?

"My wife, Geri is from Houston just like yours."

Tonye nodded, though that explained nothing. "Did something happen? What do you need from me?"

"Nothing for now," Hakeem said, sounding breathless. "But if something does happen to me, I need to know I can count on you to help her. Please, I don't have anyone else to go to that they won't know about."

Tonye glanced at the closed sliding doors and hoped no one was outside listening. "Who are 'they'? What do you mean if something happens? If you want me to help, you have to tell me everything I need to know, Hakeem."

The man smiled, but his eyes were ghostlike. "Someone's trying to kill me," Hakeem said. "And I think they might kill her too. Please, help me save Geri."

THE END.

Meet the Authors

Dee Osah is a husband-wife team with a godly passion for weaving their personal experiences into stories anyone can enjoy. They live in Houston with two young daughters, who already love to whip up compelling tales. When not writing, they enjoy analyzing the financial markets, watching K-dramas and Anime, and learning to grow food for their ever-growing family.

My Sugar in Sugar Land is Book One of the *Improbable Romance* Novels, a series within a fictional world in which the Teka Family of *Teka Legacy* resides. If you enjoyed this book, we'd love to hear from you. Please scan the QR code below to visit our website, join our newsletter, or to leave a book review. Your one review helps us and others more than you can ever imagine, so we appreciate you in advance.

Thank you for reading ***My Sugar in Sugar Land*** and stay tuned for more to come.

www.ingramcontent.com/pod-product-compliance
Lightning Source LLC
LaVergne TN
LVHW091047080826
845145LV00002B/656

* 9 7 8 1 9 6 2 4 8 5 0 1 2 *